DEDICATION

To my heart beat my soul Miracle Monet Riley. Every day that I'm allowed to be in your presence you bring me joy. I love you always.

As always, I dedicate anything I do in life to my daughter. She is the good in me. When I look over everything I have been in my life, I know that she is the reason I made it through.

I don't know why God picked me to be her mom, but what I do know is this. I will continue to dedicate my life trying to be the best mother I can be for her. My heart beats for her, my soul yearns for her, my happiness comes from her.

I never knew a love like this could ever exist, but I am blessed to be a part of a love so great nothing or no one can come between it. When my baby gets old enough to go back and read her mommy's life work, she will know that no one in this world could ever love her as much as me.

I love you with my whole being Miracle Monet Riley. Look at what your mom is doing

e is *achievable, nothing is imp* *chable*

D1414006

To any mom out there that is raising a child with Autism or any other special needs I love you. We fight a war that no other parent could imagine. I know your heart, I see your strength, I am you. Keep pushing.

To all my friends and family, I love you. I will keep pushing and being better to make you proud. One day all my wrongs will be overwhelmed by my rights. Each book I write is to show my daughter and my family, that Latoya Nicole is more than. More than what people made me out be, more than what the news made me out to be, and more than I was willing to prove to myself. On today, I know that I am MORE THAN.

To everyone that bought all fifteen books I thank you from the bottom of my heart. I hope my story reached someone and changed a life. I will continue to write and hopefully make you proud.

ACKNOWLEDGMENTS

TO MY FAMILY...

To those of you who choose to stand beside me in all of my dreams and aspirations, I thank you. It's not easy to deal with me sometimes, but you all love me just the same. I remember my publisher telling me, Toya, your family and friends aren't your readers. You think they will be the ones supporting you, but they won't. In my mind, I thought she was crazy. I just knew my people would always have my back, but I have been shown differently. There is a select few that has been on this journey with me from the beginning and I thank you from the bottom of my heart. Just know that I appreciate you and it's coming.

TO MY PEN SISTERS AND GIRLS

We have a bond like no other. This industry is cut throat, yet we manage to struggle our way to the top as we try to push each other as well. You all keep my day going and I love what each of you for different reasons, but most importantly, for loving and accepting little ol me. Ash, Paris, Panda, ZaTasha, Kb Cole, Dawn, Juanita, I love yall.

TO THE SQUAD

You girls are amazing, and I appreciate every single thing you do. You don't have to share my links, or change your profile pics, but you do. We climbing to the top, and I want you to know that I expect you to be there every step of the way.

MY TEST READERS

When I didn't believe in myself, you did, and I thank you from the bottom of my heart. ZaTasha I would never stop thanking you because I could never thank you enough. You never count me out, and I love you with all my heart Zee bae.

TO MY BESTIE

Thank you for loving me and my daughter. You said bestie this your one, claim it. I didn't believe you and look at me now. You and Zee called it. Your ass will stay on the phone with me knowing you got school the next day, all because my baby wants to send you to the moon. Kadeene be ready to kill us, but you never turn your hang up. You listen as long as I need to talk. Love you.

TO MY SIS

Kb Cole your ass has been one of my biggest fans since day one. You think every book should have been number one. Thank you for believing in me and I'm so happy to know you. I love you and keep pushing. You are awesome. Kiss Sarai for me.

TO MY COUSIN

Ash you are a pain in my backside. Lol. We can laugh and talk for hours and I am so glad to have someone I can tell my crazy stories to, even if you do think they be bad. You never say it, even when you think it. I love you and I am so glad I got to meet you. Ashton, hey boo.

MY PUBLISHER

Thank you Mz Lady P for giving me a chance. I have learned so much from you and I'll forever be happy I signed to you. Thank you for everything. I'm coming for your spot. lol

ON THE 12TH DAY OF CHRISTMAS

MY SAVAGE GAVE TO ME

LATOYA NICOLE

PROLOGUE

MODEST 2016...

Driving through the city, I been looking for this nigga June. He been hiding from my ass all week and this nigga's time was up. Everybody wanted me to let the shit go because it was Christmas, but I didn't give a fuck about the holidays.

"Hey nigga, I'm ready to go hang out and shit. We can find this nigga tomorrow. You be on some other shit."

Lando stayed on good bullshit. I swear this nigga hustled just to have money to give to the stripper bitches at KOD. This that new shit that I couldn't get with. All the work we put in out here, sacrificing our lives, his ass chooses to throw it away on these hoes.

"You can go to the club, just know your bitch ass gone be out of a job. Fuck I look like? You got this shit twisted. Keep playing pussy with your ugly ass, you gone get fucked. This shit ain't no fucking game."

"You got us chasing this nigga over five thousand dollars. That's some petty ass shit. Where that nigga Meek at?"

Looking at this nigga like he was crazy, I decided to entertain his goofy ass. My brother Meek was worse than me. Grabbing my phone, I face timed him. This nigga didn't answer until the last ring.

"What up baby bruh? You found that nigga yet?"

"Naw, not yet. We got a lil situation."

Handing my phone to Lando, I grabbed my pistol out of my waist. The nigga was actually trying to plead his case to my brother. Either he didn't want to know it, or he was turtle dumb slow. Meek was the most ruthless nigga out here in these streets. Tired of hearing the nigga whining about some bitches, I drew my hand back and knocked the lie out his ass.

"What the fuck. Meek, you better get this nigga."
Laughing, I snatched my phone back from his clown ass.

"If yall done playing around, go get my fucking money."
Hanging up the phone, I turned to Lando.

"You still want to talk to Meek?" Laughing in his face, I made a mental note of the death look this nigga was giving me. We were cool, but I didn't give a fuck about him or anybody else out here. The only nigga I knew I loved and could trust, was my big brother Meek.

He was all the fuck I needed out here. Turning the corner, I saw that nigga June, I could barely get the car in park before I jumped out. That nigga Lando was still in his feelings, and stayed in the car. Not giving June a chance to turn around, his ass was hit. Satisfied that he was gone to the other side, I ran back to my car.

When I pulled off, I made sure I was doing about seventy miles per hour. Reaching across Lando, I opened his door.

"What the fuck you doing nigga?"

"Hit me up when your bitch ass get out your feelings. Pushing his ass out of my car, I drove down some and pulled over. Closing my door. I sped off as he ran towards me. Leaving him looking at my taillights, I laughed at his goofy ass.

CHAPTER 1 MODEST

2017...

Same ol shit, just a different day. Me and my homie was sitting in the stash house counting up the money we collected. My brother Meek was cleaning shit up, so we could go all the way legit. In the meantime, somebody had to make sure shit was straight.

We did the same shit every day, and this nigga Lando talked shit every fucking time. For the most part, I ignored the shit. When his lame ass started to do the most, I would have to lay that nigga out and let him know who the fuck he worked for.

"Look, I know you don't have a girl and shit, but I do. It's the fucking holidays and you got me out here collecting money, and bagging up drugs all hours of the night. My girl gone be pissed."

That's what I meant, all the fuck he did was bitch. Ever since that nigga wifed the stripper, he been on some other shit. Who in the fuck gets in a relationship with a bitch that shows her

12

ass for a living is beyond me. This nigga be all in the front row cheering her on.

"You act like you going the fuck home. All you trying to do is run your dumb ass to the strip club, to throw that bitch all your money. Shut the fuck up. If you bag this shit up as much as you talk, we would be done."

"Don't call my girl a bitch."

"You right. Hoes get offended when you mess that shit up."

The look in his eyes let me know he wanted to try me, but he knew better. He was my nigga, but I would light his ass up and send him home to his mama as a present for the holidays. Two hours later, we were getting out of there and that nigga was pissed.

I started to keep him longer, just to be an ass. Jumping in my 2018 Bugatti Chiron, I ripped through the streets of Chicago. All the Christmas decorations had me in a fucked up mind frame. I hated this shit and it seemed like everywhere I turned, it was there.

Not really the hanging out type, and my brother was at home with his wife, I headed my ass in the house. It was a couple of niggas I fucked with, but the only nigga I trusted was my

brother Meek.

We were the only two kids my parents had, and our bond

was like no other. Meek was five years older than me, but you

wouldn't know that with how close we were. He was thirty and I

was twenty five. Everything about us was just alike, except our

feelings towards Christmas. When I was fifteen, our parents were

killed on Christmas Eve.

Meek had come home this Christmas, and I was excited as

fuck. He stayed away most of the time, because my parents didn't

approve of him being a drug dealer. He was smart as hell, and

instead of going to school, he used that shit to climb to the fucking

top. He walked in the door with all kinds of boxes to put under the

tree and I was going crazy.

"Meek Matthews, what did I tell you about trying to spoil

this boy. He don't need all of that stuff. He needs to learn how to

work for what he wants."

"Ma, get off that shit. It's Christmas. Everybody deserves to be spoiled on that day. Some of the stuff is for you and pops anyway." My father didn't say anything, he barely speaks to Meek.

"I can't wait to open my shit. This gone be the best Christmas ever."

"Modest if you don't watch your mouth. Matter fact, take your dumb ass to bed. You gone let your brother get your ass beat. Always trying to show the fuck off." My dad always took shots at Meek through me.

"Gone head, I'll be here when you wake up." Heading upstairs, I went to sleep. The next morning, I raced downstairs ready to see what Meek had gotten me, and my parents were laying there dead as fuck. My screams woke my brother up, and he came flying down the stairs. All of the presents were gone, with a lot of other shit. Somebody came in and robbed the house, and instead of just taking the shit, they killed my parents.

From that day forward, I hated the fuck out of Christmas. Laying down, I forced myself to go to sleep so that I could get those images out of my head. The shit only came back full force around this time of year. Not wanting to deal with the shit, I closed my eyes hoping sleep found me.

Even though it was Saturday, I always got up early to go run errands and shit. Grabbing a jogging suit and a hoodie, I threw on some Jays and headed to the bathroom. Rubbing coconut oil in my hands, I ran my shit through my beard. A nigga had to keep my shit moisturized. Running out the door, I was ready to start.

Jumping in my whip, I headed to the gas station. A nigga was too fly to run out of gas. Pulling in, it was cold as a bitch outside and I dreaded pumping my gas. Jogging inside, I paid for my shit and headed back out.

"Excuse me, can I pump your gas for some change?" This lil nigga had to be about six years old.

"Hell naw. Get the fuck out of my face and take your bad ass in the damn house somewhere. It's below zero out here and you got your simple ass out here begging."

Walking away, I went to the pump, started that shit, and jumped inside my car. Looking back toward the little boy, I tried my best to ignore his ass. Pulling his arms in his coat, it was obvious he was freezing. The tears could barely roll down his face, because it was so damn cold out there. Seeing him like that, the shit pissed me the fuck off. After my shit was done, I put the pump back and got ready to head out. Stopping in front of the little boy, I rolled my window down.

"Get the fuck in."

"I'm not going nowhere with you. I don't know you."

"But you knew me enough to beg for my fucking money. Get the fuck in the car." You could tell my tone scared him. Reluctantly he walked to the other side and got in.

"Show me where the fuck you live." Guiding me a few blocks down, I jumped out of my car and was pissed I was back in the cold. He led the way to his door, and walked in. His dumb ass mama in the hood with her shit open. That made me think about my parents again. Shaking that shit off, I waited for him to come back with her trifling ass.

When she rounded the corner, my dick jumped. She was pretty as fuck, and her gown was hugging her body. I knew she ain't have shit on under it, because I could see her nipples clear as

17

day. She was a pretty ass brown color, and even though she had on a bonnet, she still looked good as fuck. Her eyebrows and nails were done, and to know she had her son begging so she could be fly, pissed me off again.

"Why the fuck are you in my house?" Her nasty ass attitude had me ready to snatch her ass up.

"Why the fuck you got your lil ass son outside begging for change in below zero weather? You in this bitch cozied up in the heat and he out there freezing and shit."

"How about you stay the fuck out of my business. You don't know him, and you don't know me. I would appreciate it if you got the fuck out."

"I would appreciate it if your dumb ass acted like a mother. Trifling ass bitch."

Walking out the door, I was three fifty hot. How the fuck she mad, when I was trying to help her dumb ass out. Driving off to handle business, I tried to figure out why I was so pissed. I didn't know them, and he wasn't my fucking kid. No matter how hard I tried to shake it, I couldn't.

Heading inside the office, Meek was there going over paperwork. His ass always had this perplexed ass look on his face whenever his ass went over the numbers. You could tell some shit wasn't adding up, and his ass wasn't gone stop until he figured it out.

"Nigga what got you looking like a bitch tried to touch your asshole?" He finally looked up and realized I was in the room.

"Shut your dumb ass up. Money ain't been adding up the last couple of months and I can't figure out who the fuck shorting us."

"All the money I been collecting been straight." I always make sure I double count my shit, so I knew the shit wasn't on my end.

"I'll figure it out. Do you have all your ducks in a row? You know when the new year hits we done with this shit."

"I'm good. Have you told the crew yet?" Meek was buying up properties left and right and even though I didn't think it would bring in the same kind of money, we were going to run our own real estate business.

"Naw, we gone have a meeting one day this week. How you holding up?"

"I'm good. Your wife still got you on a curfew?" You could tell he knew I was lying.

"Modest, I know you nigga. Imma let you make it though. I'm here if you want to talk about it."

"I said I'm good damn. Leave me the fuck alone about the shit." Not even waiting on him to respond, I got up and walked out of the office. Mother fuckers always wanted to play counselor and shit. That was the last thing I wanted to talk about. I couldn't wait for this Christmas shit to be over with. That's the only time everybody wanted to talk to me about how the fuck I felt. Like they ain't dead every other fucking day of the year. Speeding off down the street, I headed back to the house. I wish I could sleep until fucking New Years.

CHAPTER 2 MALAE

Slamming my door shut, I went in the room to compose myself before I fucked Tyler up. Not only did he take his ass out of this house without me knowing, he brought a stranger in my shit. A rude one at that. I had no idea what would possess a six year old to take they ass outside and beg.

Yeah, I know shit been hard around here, but I'm the parent and I would make it work. It was times like this that I missed my child's father. Tyler was changing right before my eyes, and I had no idea what to do about it. Needing to know what the fuck he was thinking, I went to his room.

"Ty, why would you think that shit was okay? What were you doing out there?" His eyes filled with tears, forcing me to calm down.

"I heard you on the phone saying you didn't have any money and I just wanted to help you. I'm sorry, I hope Santa is still going to bring me presents." My heart broke and I was damn near speechless.

21

"Baby listen, we are going to be okay. You have to let mama handle this on her own okay?" When I knew he understood, I got up and headed to the kitchen. He had a bitch feeling like shit. This was our favorite time of year, but this year the shit was kicking my ass.

Looking around at my small ass apartment, I wanted to break down and cry. A year ago, we were living in the suburbs without a care in the world. All that shit was snatched away when he was killed. Not being able to afford the bills, we had to move back to the hood and shit been down hill since.

With all these bills and school, I barely had money to do anything else and the shit was breaking my heart. Ty had all kinds of shit on his list, but the way my account was set up, he wouldn't be able to get one. A bitch was this close to becoming Anna Nicole Smith. Glancing at the table, the bills were stacked high and the only thing keeping me from checking out was my son.

"Ma the tv not working." Knowing the lights had just been disconnected, I grabbed my phone to pay my last hundred dollars to get them back on.

"It's ok baby. They will be fixed in a minute." With tears pouring down my face, I prayed for better days.

****

Heading into work, I went straight to my boss' office. He seemed to be an asshole, but I prayed he let me pick up some extra hours. Even though I just started this job, I needed to get all I could so that I could get Ty something for Christmas. After only working here a couple of days, I was nervous as hell. My last job had budget cuts, and they let me go. Thank God I found another job so soon, but with my hours, I still wouldn't be able to Christmas shop.

"Mr. Matthews, can I talk to you for a minute?" Not even looking up, his ass was all into the papers he was looking at.

"Talk." Instead of cursing his ass out, I got my attitude in check.

"Is there any way I could pick up some extra hours. Right now, you have me as part time and I don't mind working all day."

"If I needed you all day, don't you think I would have hired you full time? There is no need for you to be here like that until after the new year." His phone rung, and just like that, his ass had dismissed me. Defeated, I headed back to my desk and I couldn't stop the tears from flowing. No matter how I looked at it, there was no way Ty could get something this year.

Even though we were broke, there was no way I was going to let our favorite holiday be ruined. At least I could do was allow him to put up the tree. That was always me and my baby father's favorite part. The music and decorating always put us in the Christmas spirit. Mr. Matthews walked out of his office, and I decided to ask one more thing of him.

"Hey boss, can we decorate the office? It's the holidays and we don't have a single thing in here to show it."

"No. If I see one decoration even outside this office, you are fired. Can you please just do what I am paying you to do? If I need anything extra, I will let you know." If I didn't need the money, I would have quit right on the spot. This nigga had me fucked up, and I knew it was no way I could work for him that long.

The door opened, and this bad ass bitch walked in. I've never seen someone so well put together. Who dresses like a fashion model in the heart of the winter? Smiling, she waved at me

and headed straight to Mr. Matthew's office. Before I could ask

her to wait, her red bottoms had disappeared inside, and the door

was closing in my face. I'm starting to think everybody on this side

of town was rude as fuck. Even though she was polite by speaking,

she knew damn well her ass wasn't just supposed to walk in there.

Hoping she didn't get me fired, I nervously waited for them to

finish.

When she walked out of the office, he grabbed her by the

ass and pulled her back to him. It wasn't until that moment, that I

realized how fine this man was. The aggressiveness about him,

would make anybody wet. Realizing I was looking like a creep

watching them kiss, I tried to find something to do. Hearing her

heels again, I knew she was about to leave.

"Hey, I'm Victoria the asshole's wife. Don't let him get to

you, it's all a front." Laughing nervously, I didn't know if I should

agree or keep my mouth shut.

"I'm Malae. He is definitely difficult. Just before you came

in, he chewed me the fuck out because I asked him to decorate the office. It takes a special kind of asshole to hate Christmas." Not expecting her to laugh so hard, I couldn't do shit but laugh with her.

"He loves Christmas. Your other boss, his brother doesn't. Now that's the real asshole, you must haven't met him yet." She laughed at the terror that was clearly showing on my face.

"Just my luck, it's two of them. I'm not gone make it." Standing up, she got ready to leave.

"You will be fine. Meek is harmless, he's just scared of me. Modest will barely come in here, but if he does, RUN. Act like you got the runs, bubble guts, or whatever you can think of. That nigga is Hell this time of year. I'll stop in to check on you from time to time, and I'll tell Meek to take it easy on you." Having some kind of relief, I sighed.

"Thank you so much."

"It was nice meeting you Malae." When she left out, I felt a little better about working here. All I had to do was avoid the one named Modest and I should be fine.

"Malae, can you come here for a minute." Hearing the tone of his voice, I may not be fine after all. He was fine, but he was scary as fuck. Everything about him screamed street nigga, but I guess that's why you can't judge a book by it's cover. When I entered his office, he kept writing and never looked at me. Victoria must have his ass shook.

"Yes, Mr. Matthews."

"Tomorrow, we are going to be at Garfield Park giving away food and stuff to families. If you can, make sure you swing by. I'll be gone for the rest of the day, so lock up when you leave. Before you walk out of that door, make sure you have the Barton deal closed. Don't accept anything less than half a mil or don't bother coming in Monday." This raggedy ass nigga got up and walked out, leaving me looking stupid.

If he is the nice one, Lord knows I don't want to meet the brother. At least we can get some food and stuff tomorrow. Since I used my last to pay the light bill, it was gone be rough as hell. Walking back to my desk, I picked up the phone to negotiate with his client. I hope they agree to the deal. I needed this job.

Thankfully, the client was willing to meet the terms. Shutting everything down, I locked up and headed home. I needed to log in to do my assignments for my real estate class. I couldn't wait until I got my license. Then I would be able to get commission, but for now, a bitch was broke without a clue as to where my next dollar was coming from.

All I could do was pray for better days as I picked Ty up from school. Something had to give, and quick.

CHAPTER 3 MEEK

You could see the fear on Malae's face every time she had to say something to me. Normally I'm not an asshole, but me and Vikki been arguing since I hired a female to run the office. She wanted me to hire some nigga named Secret. There was no way in hell I was gone be closed in with a switching ass nigga in a dress. Her popping up here, was her way of letting her presence be known.

The crazy part is, she didn't even have to do that shit. She knew damn well I would never cheat on her. My girl was a special kind of crazy. We been together since high school, and I loved everything about her ass. The first time I met her, I was dating this chick named Heather. I thought she was it for me, until the day I met Vikki.

We were in the parking lot hugged up like we always were, and this chick came out of nowhere. She stormed up to us, and I had no idea what the hell was going on. Everybody knew I was getting money, and because of that all of the chicks threw

themselves at me. None of them were bold enough to step to me

while I was with my girl though.

"You got ten seconds to get away from my man." Me and

Heather looked at this chick like she was crazy.

"Excuse me?" My girl was pissed, but the fire in the other

girl's eyes had me worried.

"Baby come on. I ain't got time for the dumb shit." That

was my weak attempt at breaking the shit up. This crazy broad

actually started counting.

"One, two, three, four." Now I'm amused because I wanted

to know what would actually happen if she got to ten. Heather

started to look worried and I knew it wasn't going to go well, but I

couldn't bring myself to stop it. When she reached ten, the mother

fucker pulled out a blade and Heather took off running. Maybe my

ass wasn't shit, but I could not stop laughing.

My girl talked so much shit, I never knew her ass was a

punk. The other girl walked back up out of breath, looking like she

was about to pass the fuck out.

"Damn that bitch fast. I'm Victoria your girl, now take me home. A bitch too tired to walk." Everybody told me I was dead wrong, but I took her home and she been my girl ever since. A nigga like me was about to be too deep in these streets. I needed a chick who could deal with the life I chose to live.

Most people felt she was an opportunist, but that was my ridah. Our lives have been damn near perfect until I told her about me leaving the street life alone. The plan was never for me to do this shit forever. See I was a smart ass nigga, and I took over these streets quick as hell. Knowing that life will eat you alive, I paved the way for me to do what I really wanted without having to work for the next nigga.

Vikki not understanding this shit, her ass wants me to be a street nigga forever. Not that her ass has a choice, come the first of the year, I'm done. My last order of business as a savage out here in these streets is to dead the nigga that's stealing from me.

Walking in the door, her ass was in the front room watching tv in heels. Since I became that nigga, her entire demeanor changed. She turned into one of them snobby ass chicks.

31

I can't remember the last time I've seen her without her heels on. If I didn't love her, everything about her would turn me off. Don't get me wrong, Vikki was my ridah, and my friend. I just preferred a chick who didn't mind wearing a pair of beat up converse, and jogging pants. My ass was so tired of hearing them damn heels click clacking all over the damn floor.

"Malae is pretty." Knowing where this conversation was leading, I got aggravated as fuck.

"I didn't know that was your type."

"You know what the hell I'm saying." Running my hands down my face, I sat on the couch preparing for this dumb ass argument.

"Look, when I hired her, I didn't care how she looked. I asked you to work in the office with me, but your ass was too good to do that."

"The fuck I look like working in a damn office when I'm a millionaire. You got me twisted." This was the part of her that I hated.

"Vikki, can you go buy a building with my money? Can you get alimony or child support from me? If I passed away, and Modest chose not to give you a dime, could you fight it in court?" She had the dumbest look on her face.

"What the fuck are you talking about Meek?"

"You're so caught up in this life your dumb ass don't have a fucking clue. Well let me break it down for you smart ass dummy. If something happens to me, you don't get a dime. If I decided to leave your ass, you won't get shit. You don't have shit to stand on but them weak ass heels you done ran the soles off of. I'm going straight for you, for us. Get on board Victoria, or all those years we been together won't mean shit."

"Who the fuck you think you talking to? Nigga I been there. What the fuck you mean if something happens to you, I won't get shit? I'm your wife." Smirking as she finally caught on, I stood up to leave the room.

"I don't trust a soul in this world, but my brother. You heard what the fuck I said." Leaving her in her thoughts, I went upstairs to jump in the shower. As the water ran over my body, I thought about my brother. I loved Christmas, but I had to take his feelings into consideration. Around the holidays, he won't even come over because of the decorations. If he knew the fancy ass shit Vikki be having up, he would see that the shit don't look like the holidays in here. It's like a damn museum. I couldn't wait until this shit was over. A nigga was stressing the fuck out.

When I walked in the room, Vikki was laid in the bed naked with just her pumps on. She actually thought she looked sexy. Sitting there playing in her pussy, she kept kicking her legs in the air. Needing to bust this nut, I climbed between her legs.

"Take those pumps off." Her neck almost snapped off as she turned to face me.

"What kind of nigga don't like to fuck a chick in sexy ass heels?"

"The kind that don't like fucking old ass bitches on the usher board. We like sexy heels, not them old lady stuffy ass pumps you been marching your ass in all damn day." Slamming my dick in her, I didn't even give her the chance to brace herself for this mother fucker.

"I said take them off." When I slammed my dick in her stomach, she kicked them mother fuckers off quick as hell.

"Slow down baby you're hurting me." Not giving a fuck about her feelings, I kept tearing them guts up. These nine inches and that curve can be a beast when I want it to be.

"Shut the fuck up and take this shit. You talk too much." Flipping her over, I shoved my thumb in her ass and slammed my dick back in. "I keep telling your ass you don't run shit. Arch your back." All she did was bury her face in the pillow, so I pushed down in the small of her back and went to work.

"Fuck. I'm about to cum." She hated when I fucked her rough like this, but she always came. Even though she was shaking, I continued my assault until I felt my nut rising up. Pulling out, I shot my seeds on her back.

"Why the fuck you keep doing that?"

"I told you I'm not having a baby until I'm out this life." Turning over, I went to sleep on her ass. I was tired of arguing.

CHAPTER 4 MODEST

Grunting as I tried to roll out of bed, I couldn't get up because this chick had her arm wrapped around me like we were Siamese assholes. Looking at her, I couldn't for the life of me remember her name or what the fuck was I thinking spending the night. Since a nigga don't cook, I went to grab some food from Hodies. She walked in looking like she had just left the club, and was all over my ass.

It's been a minute since I had some pussy, and a nigga needed to bust a nut. She was a nice looking girl, but the only thing she could get from me was a lazy ass nut. Trying to pull her arm away, the bitch tightened her grip. Glancing down at my dick, I still had on my condom. Pulling it off, I slapped her ass in the face with it like three times. She finally started to stir.

"Good morning baby. How long you been up?" This hoe was delusional.

"Bitch if you don't let me the fuck up. I got somewhere to be, and you got a nigga in here like a kidnapped victim. Move!"

"Nigga you tried it. You here because you wanted to be." She was three fifty hot.

"No bitch, I'm here because your strong arm ass got my neck on lock." Removing her arm, she smacked her lips as I got dressed. Grabbing the condom, I hit her in the face with it just because I felt like it.

"Asshole." Thinking better of it, I walked back to the bed and snatched my shit. Jumping in my whip, I sped the fuck off. Letting my window down, I threw the condom out the window. I would rather get a bird pregnant, than her ass. She looked unstable enough to be a turkey baster. Heading to my crib, I needed to get dressed for this bullshit at the park.

Even though I hated the holidays, we did this shit every year on the 1st of December. Twenty five more days and my life would be back to normal. Pulling up to my house, I ran in and handled my business. Making sure I was fly, and warm, I headed to the park.

When I pulled up, I knew my brother tried to accommodate me. There wasn't a decoration in sight. Even though I was tired of his ass pressing me about it, I was happy as fuck he did that shit.

Seeing that everybody was already here, I jumped out and headed over. They were setting up, and I fell in line.

"What up nigga. Where you been?" Meek was extra as fuck when it came to me during the holidays. I know he means well, but I would rather a mother fucker just let me be.

"Fucking. Damn you wanna see the video?" Smacking me in the head, he continued loading the food on the table.

"I don't need to see the video, you got nut all in that dry ass beard. Dumb ass nigga."

"You tried that shit. You know I don't eat pussy. Shit ain't sanitary." All the niggas started laughing.

"Get your young ass out of here. That shit taste better than anything you could ever put in my face. Your dumb ass better grow up. No wonder you can't keep a bitch, nigga out here having teenage sex." Lando thought he was funny, since everybody laughed at his ass.

"Nigga how you know what your bitch shit taste like? You down there eating the whole city nut. Your bitch fuck for a living and at the end of the night you slurping her shit down. Who the goofy? You paying her, to suck another nigga's nut." You could tell he wanted to hit me, but he knew better. "When you come for me, make sure you in the right fucking lane my nigga."

"You do be half fucking though. Your ass barely move in the pussy. I walked in on this mother fucker one day, his ass was just standing there, and the bitch had sweat her wig off trying to get her nut." I knew Meek was just trying to lighten the mood, but he wasn't lying.

"Fuck yall. I know how to fuck. These hoe ass bitches ain't getting all that from me. If I could just stick the tip in and get my nut, I would." Everybody laughed, but I was dead ass. "Call that shit tip and dip."

"Something wrong with you, help me grab these presents and shit. People starting to come." Meek loved giving just as much as I did. In our mind, the person that robbed and killed our parents was in a desperate situation. By us helping them, we could be saving someone else's life. Maybe one of these niggas was gone go rob somebody tonight because they didn't have shit to eat. Or they didn't have shit to buy they kids, but after today, they would. That was the only reason I partook in this shit.

When the park started to get crowded, I branched off to the side. Sitting on the truck, I watched the smiles on their faces and I wish I could feel like that again. Remembering how much I loved tearing the paper wondering what was underneath, I felt my eyes start to sting. This was why I didn't like the holidays. It made me feel shit I didn't want to.

"Mommy, look at all this stuff the man gave me." Hearing his voice, I looked up and saw the little boy that was begging me for change. This bitch looked good as fuck, but out here getting our shit like she was in need. These were the kind of mother fuckers I hated. Getting up, I headed over.

"Did you say thank you." She was smiling as she held a food box. I was about to wipe that shit right off her face.

"Not only do you send your son to stand on corners to beg for you, but now you out here taking away from a mother fucker in need. You as trifling as they come." She turned to me still smiling.

"Ty, go play in the bouncy houses. I'll be over to get you in a few."

"Okay mommy, can you hold my presents." Grabbing his stuff, she made sure he was out of ear shot before she turned back to me.

"I don't know what the fuck your deal is, but I really don't give a fuck. You wanna sit your dumb ass on a high horse and judge a mother fucker because you out here giving to the less fortunate. None of the shit matters if the shit ain't genuine. So, fuck you and get the fuck out of my face."

"Shut the fuck up. All that rah rah shit don't move me. You trifling, and that's the bottom line. I hope you choke on that fucking food. Dumb ass broad." I was about to go harder on the dumb hoe, but Meek walked up.

"Fuck are yall doing. Today ain't about that. Malae, we ran out of toys, and it's a family that I know needs it, just came. Let me get this for them." She smiled, but the look in her eyes damn near broke me. It wasn't until that moment, I realized her ass was one of those in need. She still was trifling as fuck for sending her son out there to beg for her dumb ass though. Meek took the gifts, and walked off. She tried hard as fuck to not let those tears fall.

I stood back and watched her until Meek walked back to her needing her food box as well. Walking over to them, I tried to intervene.

"Nigga how you gone give somebody something and then take it back?" She almost looked grateful.

"Because, its someone who needs it. We bought extra shit this year and still ran out."

"She too slow to say it, but she wants the shit nigga."

"Fuck you. I don't need you talking for me." This chick was unbelievable. Here I was trying to help her, but fuck it.

"If you ever speak to your boss in that manner again, you will not only be out of a job, but you will regret ever meeting me." She worked for us? I was about to give her a smug look when

Meek burst her bubble, but the tears actually came down her face this time.

"I'm so sorry, I didn't know he was Modest." She turned to me to apologize, and for the first time in a long time, I felt like shit. "I'm sorry Mr. Matthews. I'm just going to leave, this was a disaster." Before I could tell her it was okay, she took off running.

"Bro when we hire her, and how you pull that off with Vikki?"

"Fuck Vikki, and the other day."

"What you know about her?" Giving me a strange look, a smile crept up his face.

"Nothing really. She is in school for her license, and she good at her job when she not being extra. Mother fucker been there two days and asking for extra hours." His ass missed all the damn signs. Malae was struggling, and needed the money. Before we could finish our conversation, Vikki came trotting across the park in some damn heels. I couldn't believe my brother stayed with her this long, she was not this nigga's type. This mother fucker gave my ass an air kiss and pulled Meek away.

Looking around the park, I tried to find Malae. She was nowhere in sight. Even though she got away today, I knew where she worked. I was going to make sure I started stopping by the office more often. Even though I wasn't trying to fuck with her, I wanted to make up for what my brother did today. That's if she came back to work. Jumping in my car, I left and went to make my rounds. I did my good deed for today, and now it was time to get what mother fuckers owed us. Knowing somebody was stealing from us, it was time I paid more attention to how mother fuckers was moving. Starting with that nigga Lando.

CHAPTER 5 VICTORIA

Getting dressed to go to the park, I had an attitude out of this world. First finding out Meek fucked up ass had all his money going to his brother, and now I had to go deal with these bums and kids. I have no idea why my husband thought it was okay to give our money away to a bunch of mother fuckers we didn't know.

Meek's family was never broke, they were what we called comfortable. My family was dirt poor, and I knew that I was destined to be rich. I've always thought I was better than the next even when I didn't have shit. I was Victoria McIntyre. Daughter of a bitch who worked at Wendy's all her life, and my father was a custodian. A fancy fucking way to say janitor. That wasn't going to be my life.

The minute I laid eyes on Meek, I knew I had to have him. He was a brown complexion and he was fine. He wore his hair low back then, but now he wears it in a low box. The sexiest thing about him was his mystery. He had a versatile look, so you couldn't tell if he was a street nigga or a mother fucker that worked. After seeing him in all the latest shit at sixteen, it wasn't hard to figure out what he did. That was a nigga I needed on my team. After I got his lil girlfriend out of the way, I scared off any bitch that looked his way. He was mine, and nobody would come in between that.

From the moment we started dating, I haven't wanted for anything. Not ever having to work, my life was finally going in the direction I knew it would. He was bringing in more money than I could count, and I was happy as hell. Until the nigga hit me with the going straight bullshit. He even had the nerve to ask me to work. What the fuck I look like. Knowing where this shit was headed, I formed a plan to keep me living the life I was used to.

Knowing I wasn't his beneficiary kind of fucked that up, but I had a plan b. Nobody would have me going back to nothing. Don't get me wrong, I loved Meek. I'm just no longer in love with him. I wanted the bad boy, and the fast life. That wasn't him anymore. This nigga be coming in all early wanting to watch movies and go on dates. I be wanting to scream, nigga if you don't get your ass on the block and go get our money. Of course I can't, so I have to pretend like I'm happy in love and shit. Our life has been boring as hell since he decided to walk away from the streets. Not knowing how much we had, I had to ensure I didn't go broke when his ass go under. There was no way real estate could bring in the type of money I had grown accustomed to. Grabbing my ringing phone, I answered for my side nigga.

"Hey what's up?"

"You on the way?" Sliding my feet in my Chanel pumps, I grabbed my keys and headed downstairs.

"I'm on the way now."

"Aight bet." Hanging up, I jumped in my Audi truck and headed towards the park. Now that I thought about it, all of my cars and the house was in Meek's name. He thought he was gone leave me high and dry, he had me fucked up.

As soon as I pulled up, I saw him all in the lil bitch face that he hired. She seemed cool, but I didn't trust no bitch around my man. Until I had all my ducks in a row, he was mine and I would stop at nothing to keep it that way. Watching her run off in tears, I knew my pussy still had some power. He was sprung, and that nigga would never leave me. If I was a smart bitch, I would be happy with the life I lived. Unfortunately, I was a mother fucker that wanted it all. Meek needed to get on board, or his ass was going to lose it all. Putting my game face on, I walked up to Modest and hugged it out.

"Babes, let's talk." Pulling Meek away, I could tell he was still mad from last night. "Do you think it's smart to be spending this kind of money on these people when you about to be penny pinching?"

"For some reason, you keep trying a nigga. Don't forget who the fuck you are talking to, and for your information. I won't be penny pinching, but you will."

"All of a sudden, it's your money this and your money that. We started this shit together, don't you forget that."

"Have you ever stood on a fucking block? Bagged up some work? Kill a nigga because they were stealing from us? Vikki all you have ever done is reap the benefits. I've never given a fuck about that, because if I have it, my girl got it. Shit started changing when you started acting like the only thing that matters is money.

48

Now we are here to give to the less fortunate, I'm not in the mood for your shit."

"All you want to do now is throw our life and our money away. What the fuck are you doing Meek?" This nigga was stepping on my feet hard as hell.

"You forgot what it's like to climb your way out the mud. I thought you might need to be reminded." Walking off, he left me stuck. Literally. It took me a couple of minutes to get my heels out that damn dirt, and I was pissed. This nigga was changing, and I didn't like it one bit. Heading over to my side nigga, I was ready to get out of there.

"Meet me in thirty minutes." I'm over this faking shit, it was time to put our plan all the way in motion. This would be another Christmas he would never forget.

CHAPTER 6 MALAE

Walking into the office, I wanted to be anywhere but here. These niggas were crazy and mad disrespectful, but I needed the practice and I damn sure needed the money. If I had my choice, I wouldn't be anywhere near the Matthew brothers.

I had never been so humiliated in my life. The one nigga I hated had to be the boss I've never seen. Modest irked my entire soul, and now I can't say shit to this nigga or I will lose my job. I'm pretty sure Meek was threatening me in another way as well, but I would hope he wasn't that type of man.

Now Modest was all street. Everything about his ass screamed hood nigga. His aura let you know he was a savage, and a year ago that would have turned me on. My baby's father lived that life, and I will never do that shit again. When his friends came to tell me he was dead, my soul was shattered. If it wasn't for Ty, I would have given up a while ago.

My life has been one hell of a shit show ever since. Slamming my shit down on my desk, I started on my work. I could tell Meek wasn't here yet, and I was glad. When that nigga took my baby's toys, and food back, I wanted to slap his ass to sleep. Not wanting anybody to know how bad my situation was, I had to fight to keep the tears from falling. Ty was so disappointed when we got home, he thought he did something wrong for them to take his stuff back.

Those would have been the only gifts Ty would have had for Christmas, but at least he would have had something. Now I was back to square one. Times like this, I wish I had family to call on for help. If I had any, I didn't know who they were. I've been in and out of foster homes my entire life. All the kids used to pick on me because I didn't have shit. They would tease me every day. "Here comes the dirty ass orphan." One day I was going in the store to steal me some snacks, and a group of niggas were out there playing dice.

"You know damn well you ain't got no money to pay for shit in that mother fucker. Come here baby, you ain't gotta steal. If you give me some head, I'll buy your shit." I've never been a bitch, but I couldn't stop the tears that flowed from my eyes.

51

Everyone out there were staring waiting to see my response. When I locked eyes with my baby's father, my heart fluttered.

"Don't be talking to my girl like that. I'll fade your ass nigga." He defended me, took me in the store, and bought me whatever I wanted. After that, we were inseparable. For nine years, he was my world, my protector, and the streets took his life. I miss his ass every day, and I know Ty do as well. Hearing the door open, I wiped my eyes and continued working.

"Good morning Malae." Shocked, I almost forgot to speak back. This was the first time Meek had spoken to me.

"Good morning Mr. Matthews. The deal was sealed for seven hundred thousand, the papers will be signed and faxed over today."

"Good work." He nodded towards the door, and walked in his office. Looking over my shoulder, Modest was standing there. Not in the mood for his shit, I kept working. Hearing him walk in and out the door, piqued my curiosity. Turning around, the empty desk by the door was filled with food. This nigga had me fucked up. If he thought for one second I was going to be his charity case after the way he talked to me, he had another thing coming. Jumping up from my desk, I went over to him and slapped the smirk off his face.

"How dare you? You think I'm some bum you can talk down to, and then come throw some charity at me and make it better. I will starve before I take a piece of bread from your arrogant ass. Fuck you and this food." Knowing I was fired after this stunt, I snatched my shit and ran out of the door.

With tears running down my face, I jumped in my car and headed home. The rumbling in my stomach slapped me back to reality. I was in no position to turn down anything. My pride had my ass hungry as fuck without a clue as to what we would eat for dinner. It was okay for me to say fuck me, but I shouldn't have done that to my son.

As a parent, we have to do things we don't want to do in order to make sure our kids were straight. With that in mind, I headed to the store, and prayed I didn't get caught. Sliding some peanut butter in my purse, I grabbed a loaf of bread, some jelly, and some chips. Throwing all the items in my purse, I ran the fuck out of there as fast as I could. Heading to Ty's school, all I could do was cry. I hope I was able to find another job soon, or we would be homeless as well. As soon as he got in the car, he started with the questions.

"Can I have McDonald's?" Wiping a tear away, I cleared my throat.

"Not today baby."

"We haven't had McDonald's since daddy left. Ooh mommy, can I have an Xbox for Christmas? All the kids are getting one. I want one. Can I have one?" More tears fell, as my heart broke.

"We'll see baby."

"Ok." When we got in the house, I pulled the stuff out of my purse. This was going to be breakfast, lunch, and dinner until I figured something out. Lying down, I got a thirty minute nap in. Hearing a knock on my door, I wondered who the hell it could be. Peeking out, I didn't see anyone, and I opened it with caution. No one was there, but it was food everywhere.

Seeing a note on the door, I grabbed it.

"Sorry for being an ass. Please take it, and we will see you at work tomorrow. M"

No longer willing to let pride stand in the way, I grabbed the food inside. My ass cried the entire time. It was so much stuff, I barely had room for it all. Modest may be a jerk, but it's a gentle side to him as well. Thanking God for his blessings, I pulled out the pots and started cooking my son a real dinner.

Back in the holiday spirit, I pulled the tree and decorations out. Turning on my music, me and Ty put up the tree while we waited on dinner to get done. It was beginning to look and feel a lot like Christmas, even though we didn't have any presents, I would thank God for what we did have.

"Mommy why do you cry so much? Are you sad" Not realizing I was crying until he asked me that, I wiped my eyes and smiled at him.

"This time mommy is crying because she is happy. Your daddy would be smiling at us right now if he was here. I want you to know something. Even when you don't have what you want, it's okay to be happy for what you do have.

Just know that mommy loves you and it's going to be okay. We have each other and that is the most important thing. Do you understand?"

"Yes, but Santa will help you on Christmas. That's why I've been extra good." Knowing he still didn't understand, I just kissed him on his head. Going into the kitchen, I fixed our plates and was grateful to have a home cooked meal.

CHAPTER 7 MEEK

"How in the hell did you fuck it up this time?" Modest had told me how I missed all the signs with Malae. In his mind, she was in need, and he was determined to help her. He said it was to keep her son from going out doing something stupid, the lil nigga was six. He liked Malae and he didn't want to admit it. If she needed help, why wouldn't she ask?

This nigga had me late for work going to the grocery store grabbing all this food for a chick that didn't look like she missed a meal a day in her life. Her ass was fat as hell. Six hundred dollars later, we were putting all that shit in the truck. Now, because somehow he managed to piss her off again, we were out here in the cold taking them to her door.

"Man all I did was bring the shit in the office. She slapped the shit out of me, and ran out before I could say one word. She lucky I didn't wipe her crooked ass eyebrows off." Yeah, he liked her.

"Yet here we are again. If she doesn't want it, why are we here? You gone make her take the shit?"

"We here because it's a child involved. She can let pride get in the way, but I won't." Laughing as he tripped down the stairs and dropped his bags, I wish my hands weren't full. I would have recorded his ass.

"Nigga you about to kill yourself for a girl that don't want this shit. If I drive by here in the morning and this shit still on the porch, I'm fucking you up. We finally finished and headed back to the car.

"Hold on." I laughed as he wrote out a note and ran back up the stairs. My baby brother didn't see it yet, but he liked her. I wouldn't push the issue, or he would back away. Anything that made him feel, he stayed away from it. This was the first time I saw him show interest to anybody, and I was happy for him. Malae would be good for him, but she would have to tread lightly.

Running back to the car, he got in out of breath. When I put the car in drive he stopped me.

"Wait to see if she takes it." We watched from the car, as she opened the door and looked around. The look of gratitude that came across her face had me feeling good and it wasn't even my idea. She smiled as she read the note. Once she started to grab the items inside, I pulled off. When I looked over and saw Modest smiling, I chose not to say a word. He needed this, and I prayed he didn't fight the shit.

****

Vikki didn't come in til late last night. I guess she was still pissed, but I didn't give a fuck. What kind of woman would rather have her nigga jeopardizing his life every day, over stability? If I got her pregnant, and left, she couldn't even get child support. Women was supposed to be smarter than men. All she cared about was status and money.

Throwing on my Ferragamo suit and loafers, I left out and headed to the office. When I got in, Malae wasn't there, and the aggravation set in. Even though she had my brother touching on his feelings again, their bullshit was fucking with her job performance. Ready to call and tell her ass to not worry about coming in anymore, my phone rung. It was Malae.

"I'm so sorry Mr. Matthews, but I'm having car troubles this morning. I'm trying to get there now." Since it wasn't anything pressing for her to do, it was no big deal.

"I'll leave out and come get you."

"Thank you so much. I really appreciate that." You could tell she was happy she wasn't about to lose her job, and it made me wonder if Modest's theory was right.

"Malae, be ready." Hanging up, I grabbed my keys ready to walk out when the door opened. This girl walked in, but she looked lost. Taking in her appearance, she didn't seem to be house shopping. It actually looked like she just got off the couch, and decided to come here. Wearing a pair of Ugg boots, some leggings, jacket, and beanie. I had to admit she was cute as hell even in this simple attire.

Light brown in complexion, her eyes drew me in. She had this confidence about her, and you could tell she didn't care what anyone thought of her. Her ass sitting high in her leggings didn't help the hard on I was getting.

"Can I help you?" Walking up to me, she shook my hand.

"Mr. Matthews I assume. I'm Akina."

"Nice to meet you. Are you looking to buy a house?" She had this unsure look for the first time, and it made me want to know what had her second guessing herself.

"I really want to, but I'm not sure if I can without a loan. I'm trying not to go that route if I don't have to." It dawned on me that I was supposed to be on the way to get Malae.

"Can you give me a moment." Grabbing my phone, I called my brother.

"Hey I need you to swing by and pick up Malae. She's having car troubles and I have a client."

"Aight. I'm on the way now." Just the fact he didn't give me a hard time, I knew he liked her. Turning my attention back to Akina, I knew there wasn't a house on my listings she could afford on her own, but I wasn't ready to let her go.

"Let's head in my office and look at some things." Out of nowhere, she took my hand and followed me in. That was an odd gesture, and when she realized it, she let my hand go.

"I'm so sorry. It's just my nerves, and I didn't mean to do that." Seeing the embarrassed look in her eyes, I tried to ease her mind.

"It's fine really. Would it help if I accidentally grabbed your ass, we would be even?" When she laughed, I knew I had broken the ice. "I'm serious, I'll even let you slap me for doing it."

"Stop it, you are not grabbing my ass. Anyway, I'm not looking to spend more than a hundred thousand. I really don't want to be in the hood, but I know that it's hard to find a house in the suburbs with that amount." Knowing she said she didn't want to go through the bank, I wondered how she had saved up so much money.

"You have that much money saved?" The look on her face told me her story was deeper. Tears threatened to fall, but she held it together.

"Yeah. So what do you have?" Pretending to pull up some listings, I thought of anything I could, to keep her from walking out of my office. I wanted to keep her there as long as I could. There was no way I could cross the line with her, but I wanted to know her story. One thing was for certain, I would have to learn it quick. If Vikki even sensed another woman being around me, she would be up here trying to stab her ass.

"This may take a while to find something in your range. Do you have some time?"

"I have nothing but time." My dick jumped, but I had to tell him to simmer down. There would be no fucking, but it didn't hurt to imagine my dick sliding inside her pretty ass lips. Akina had my attention, even if it was only for one day.

CHAPTER 8 MODEST

Getting out of the bed, I threw on my jogging pants and Tims. Looking over at the bed, the two asses in the air almost made me lay back down. They had put on quite a show last night. Even though they weren't gay, when they realized I didn't eat pussy, they did each other knowing that was the only way they would get it done.

They didn't know what they were doing, but the sight alone would get any nigga dick hard. The shit almost went left when one of them tried to get up and kiss me. I almost slapped her tongue down her throat. If I didn't eat pussy, what would make the dumb broad think I would want it in my mouth. They still got the lazy fuck, but I nutted strong. While I fucked one, the other sucked my balls. The way my nut shot out, you would think I had put in work.

"Hey, get up." One looked at the clock and groaned.

"Check out is not until twelve. Get back in bed and I promise to make it worth your while."

"What the fuck did I just say? You can stay if you want, your ass better have some money. I will leave out this bitch and not pay shit."

"Damn, can you at least take us to breakfast?" Pointing towards the other girl, I nodded.

"You better eat real quick while I'm in here brushing my teeth. Hurry the fuck up, you ain't got long." Hearing the girl suck her teeth when the other asked was she gone do it, almost took me out. After I finished my hygiene check, I walked out the room and they were still slurping each other up. Grabbing my shit, I headed out.

They thought I was playing, but they was gone learn today. Stopping by the clerk, I let him know they were going to pay when they checked out. Laughing, I jumped in my whip and headed to Malae. You would think I would be trying to stay away from her mean, trifling ass.

When she slapped me, it took everything in me not to pistol whoop her lil ass. The fact that I didn't, and I still wanted to help her. Knowing how I felt about Christmas, I knew it was just my emotions all over the place. Either way, I would do my good deed and move the fuck around. The way I judged her was wrong, after I make it up to her ass, I would leave her be. That's what I told myself until I saw her walking to my car.

She had on this tight pencil skirt and heels. The shit was hugging her and all I could think about, was trying to squeeze my dick inside of it. Realizing it was me, you could see her face expression changed. She hated my ass, and I didn't have anybody to blame but myself. I was me through and through. Either you accepted me for the nigga I was, or move around.

"Hey Mr. Matthews. I thought it would be your brother. He told me he was on the way." The way she called me by my last name made me want her. Any other chick that wanted me, only saw Modest the street nigga. They didn't realize it was much more to me thanks to my brother.

"A client came in, and he asked me to come. If you got a problem with it, you can always get on the bus." Pulling over to the curb, I waited for her to decide. I'm not with the shits, and she would learn that soon enough. You could tell she wanted to hit me, but if she tried that shit again, she was in for a rude awakening.

"Do you always have to be an asshole?"

"Yup, again. Would you like to get your ride to work or are you getting the fuck out? Time is money, and we both know you can't pay me for my shit." As soon as the words left my mouth, I regretted it. She didn't even try to fight me. Climbing out of my car, she slammed my door and stood on the bus stop. Knowing I had pushed her over the edge, I parked and got out.

"Look I'm sorry. I never had to be nice to someone before. Everybody know how I am, and they accept it. You're the only one that gives me a hard time."

"Fuck your time, we both know I can't pay for it. Now if you will excuse me, my ride is here." The bus pulled up and she walked on. Trying to rectify the situation, I took a deep breath and climbed on with her. As she dug through her purse, we both knew she didn't have the money to pay for the ride. Pulling out a hundred, I handed it to the driver.

"Look, I don't carry small bills, but this should cover our fare. We good?" Pocketing the money, he nodded, and I followed her.

"Would you just leave me the fuck alone? Everything you do for someone; do you have to throw it back in their face? The shit is hurtful, and I don't deserve it. You don't know me, and you don't know my story. Just please, leave me the fuck alone."

"Everyone has a story. Just because it's not evident, don't mean it's any less relevant than the next. I have never apologized to anyone, but I did to you. What I said was wrong, and I know that. This time of year makes me meaner than I already am." Her look softened, and I was glad. It felt like a nigga was begging, and I definitely don't do that shit.

"What's your story?"

"You think we about to have a heart to heart on this funky ass bus?" Seeing that disgusted look come back, I tried a different angle. I couldn't help her if she hated me. "If you promise to cook me dinner tonight, I'll tell you."

"Deal. I can't believe you got on the bus." Looking around at the crazy looking mother fuckers, I was starting to regret it.

"Why you need a ride anyway. What's wrong with your car?" You could tell her ass was about to lie. "The real reason."

"It was repossessed last night while I was sleep. Got up this morning and it was gone." This girl was always fighting back tears. Shit was heart breaking to see one person go through so much.

"How do you know they took it? What if somebody stole it? How do you know where it is?"

"Because I haven't paid the note in four months. Just let it go okay."

"One last question, how are you going to pick your son up? Is the father in his life?" Seeing the tears actually fall, I regretted not letting it go.

"I hadn't thought about that, and his father is deceased. He got killed a year ago." All I wanted to do was wrap my arms around her. My ass sitting here crying over some shit that happened to me nine years ago, and she was going through hell while dealing with a recent death. I don't know why, but that shit touched the fuck out of a nigga. Even if we couldn't stand each other, I knew I would help her.

Seeing the office, I got happy as hell. The bus smelled like ass and Cheetos, I had no idea how people could do that shit every day. Getting off the bus, I watched her walk into the building. That ass was on swoll, and my dick was telling me it wanted inside. Knowing we couldn't cross that line, I said a quick prayer and headed in the office. When I walked in Meek's office, he was in there smiling, and laughing like this girl was his best friend. He didn't even notice I was there.

"What's going on here?" The nigga looked like he was caught with his dick down her throat.

"This is a Akina, she's looking for a house." Smiling, it was my turn to fuck with him.

"Seems like she looking for more than that. Where the fuck you come from? Come correct when it comes to my brother. Trust me, you don't want to see my other side come out." She stood up.

"That's my cue to leave. I'll call you when I make my decision. It was nice meeting you." She looked my way. "Wish I could say the same about you." I heard her mumble something about me being a crazy ass nigga or some shit like that before she walked out the door.

"Nigga what's wrong with you?" Shrugging my shoulders, I grabbed his keys.

"Nothing. I just don't trust when new people pop up out of nowhere. The bitch will get the side eye from me until I know better. I'm surprised Vikki didn't sense a chick sniffing around her man. Ready to fight in them Sunday school ass pumps. I hate them mother fuckers." He laughed, cus he knew the shit was true.

"I swear it be looking like she about to walk up on me and tell me to spit my gum out. No chewing in church." We both fell the fuck out.

"Don't ask, but I need Malae's last name and your truck for a few hours. I'll drop it back off." Heading out after getting the info, I went to make Malae's day a little better.

CHAPTER 9 AKINA

Walking into Meek's office, was the best decision I made in a long time. No one knew how hard it was for me to get out of my bed every day, and move on with life as if nothing was wrong. These last few months have been the worse, and it took everything in me not to check out. Walking in my door, I looked at the pictures on the wall and broke down. This happened every day, and it was half the reason I was losing my mind. Holding Gabbie's picture, I broke down and the thoughts came flooding back as it does every night.

"Mommy, my chest hurts." I heard her, but I was almost done with my presentation. I was Akina James, the youngest in my company. A junior partner at an advertising firm, I was working like a dog to become senior partner at the end of the month. My deadline was in thirty minutes, and I just needed a few more moments for the finishing touch.

"I'll be there in one minute baby." Five minutes later I was hitting send. Feeling accomplished, I headed to the room to see

what was wrong with Gabbie. My baby girl was seven years old, and she was all that I had. Her father couldn't take a strong black woman on the rise, and he thought it was okay to leave. The bastard hadn't called, or seen Gabbie in five years. Not a Christmas card, nothing.

Walking in her room, she was passed out on the floor with her pump in her hand. She had asthma and now I was kicking my ass for not coming to see what was wrong.

"Gabbie baby get up. Mommy will take you to the hospital. Come on baby." The tears fell as I dialed 911. It didn't take long for the ambulance to come, and I was grateful for that. Hopefully they could help her, and not have to take her to the hospital.

Moving out of their way, I allowed them to work on my baby. From CPR to breathing machines. Nothing stopped them from pronouncing her dead on arrival. Everything went black, and in that moment, my world ended.

As I did every night, I held her picture crying and apologizing.

"Mommy is so sorry baby. I should have come when you called me. I miss you every second of every minute. I need you so much, please come back. Please baby, mommy is sorry." Breaking down, I fell to the floor and cried my eyes out. This was the reason I wanted a house. The memories were too much for me, but I didn't want to spend all of my savings, or her insurance money on a house. There was no way I would ever go back to work after this. I would need this money to live. As my heart ached and cried out for her, my phone kept going off. Pulling myself up to get it, I looked at the name and saw that it was Meek. It was as if he knew I needed someone to snap me out of this breakdown.

Meek: Looking up other choices for you. Wyd?

Me: Nothing, just sitting here thinking.

Meek: About what?" Not knowing what to say, I didn't respond. As the tears found their way down my face again, all I could do was ask God why. My phone went off again.

Meek: Can I come over? As if God was giving me a shoulder to lean on, I agreed.

Me: Yes. After sending him the address, I got up and showered. Needing to get my thoughts and emotions in check, I did the best I could. Hearing the door, I threw on my shorts and tank, but I threw my robe on as well. As soon as I opened the door, it was as if he knew something was wrong. Seeing the concerned look in his eyes, the tears came flowing again. All of the prepping was for nothing. Once his arms wrapped around me, I broke down.

After I finally calmed down, I was able to sit down and explain to him what was going on. When he looked at me, I didn't see pity in his eyes like most people. They treated me like I was an invalid. Maybe I was one, but that was the reason I never visited my family. Everyone wanted me to just move on with my life, and when they noticed I couldn't, they started treating me like a damn handicap. Waiting on him to speak, I dropped my head hoping he didn't think I was a monster. When he didn't say anything, I closed my eyes knowing I had just fucked this up.

"Father God I come to you right now on behalf of Akina. You said that all we had to do is ask, and right now I'm asking for healing. You have already provided her with the strength that she

75

needs to try and move forward, even if she doesn't see it. I'm coming to you now asking for you to mend her broken heart. Allowing her to forgive herself, and know that when something is your will, it shall be done. We may not know why you chose to take Gabbie home, but I ask that you take care of the ones she left behind. When times get to hard for her to move forward, carry her. When she feels weak, wrap your arms around her Lord. She needs you in this confused state, and I ask that you give her the strength to accept your will. In Jesus name I pray, amen."

When I opened my eyes, the tears flowed, but it wasn't from hurt or pain. I have never in my life had a man to pray for me, and it moved me in ways I could never understand. This stranger, this man I met on today. Helped me in ways, no one has ever tried to. Hugging him, his arms went around me strong and tight. It was then that I took in his scent. Nothing was more sexier than a man that smelled good. Looking up to his eyes, I knew he wanted me.

It's been years since I wanted a man, and I damn sure had no intentions of dating one now. It wasn't what I wanted, but in this moment, Meek was what I needed. Leaning up to kiss him, I

76

melted against his sexy ass lips. Them mother fuckers had my shorts wet as hell, and I was kicking my own ass for not wearing panties. I was so lost in him, I didn't hear what he said. When he leaned back from me, he repeated it.

"Akina I'm married." Stepping back, I should have known my damn luck wasn't that good.

"I'm sorry. I'll call if I decide to get a house." He walked over to me, and I knew I should have pushed him back. I just felt so safe in his arms.

"It's okay babes. I should have told you, but no more sad shit. Come on, let's go watch a movie."

"Like what?"

"Not no girly ass shit. Your ugly ass done cried enough. Find some gangsta shit." We laughed and watched movies for hours. Even though he belonged to someone else, it felt like he belonged here with me.

CHAPTER 10 MALAE

Packing up my belongings, I was ready to leave for today. Knowing I had to be on the bus to get Ty, I was leaving a little early since Meek wasn't here. I was surprised to see another woman in his office. She looked entirely different from Victoria. They were like night and day. If he was messing with them both, it would be hard to tell his type. Modest left out of the office, and only came back to give Meek his keys and he was gone again.

It didn't bother me since I knew I was going to see him later. I couldn't believe I was going to have dinner with this mean ass nigga, but that's how bad I wanted to know his story. In the position I'm in, I wouldn't want to throw away the dinner I just made last night. Modest didn't look like the type that would appreciate left overs, so I would cook him something new.

****

Knowing Meek wasn't coming back, since he had been gone for a couple of hours now. I shut everything down, and locked up. When I turned around, my car was sitting there. How in the fuck? I know it was my car, because I had Ty's baby shoes

hanging from my mirror. Walking over, I was in shock trying to

figure out how the fuck it got here. On the glass was a note, and

my heart fluttered as I read it.

I'm sorry for what I said earlier, this is my way of making it

up to you. Hope this helps, it's one less thing you have to worry

about. See you at dinner. M

Was this nigga telling me he paid off my car? Grabbing my

keys, I climbed inside and got my phone out. Calling the car

dealer, I gave them my info and sure as shit stank, I had a zero

balance. How did he do that? Even though me and Modest couldn't

be together, I looked towards heaven and thanked God for his

blessings. This took a huge weight off my shoulders, but this time I

refused to cry. Smiling all the way to Ty's school, I was going to

cook him a great meal, that's the least I could do.

Dinner was smelling good, and I was in a great mood. I

decided on making him Shrimp Scampi, steak, salad, and garlic

bread. Making sure everything was good, I checked on Ty.

Hearing the knock on the door, I had to check myself at how happy I got and walked slower. Opening the door, this nigga was standing there looking daddyish. Why did he have to go home, and come back looking like come here bitch and suck this dick. Nervously, I moved back and let him in.

"Hey, the food is done are you ready to eat?" He seems just as nervous as me.

"What's up, and yeah a nigga can eat." He sat at the table, and I went to fix his food. Ty had already eaten, and he was in his room watching tv. Piling the food on, I turned to sit the plate in front of him. This nigga jumped up, and walked out. He actually had the nerve to slam the door. Standing there in disbelief, I could not believe him. This nigga made me waste my food, and I was done playing these games with him. Modest could choke on his own spit, and I wouldn't pat his fucked up ass on the back. Hearing my phone sound off, I grabbed it. Seeing a number I didn't recognize, I opened the text.

773-578-5955: Can you bring my plate, a soda, and your ass down to my car?

Me: What the fuck kind of games are you playing? You can come upstairs and eat like a normal person.

773-578-5955: Look, you know I'm not good at this shit. If you bring your mean ass downstairs, everything will make sense. You said you wanted my story, I'm trying to give it to you. Just not up there.

Me: Okay I'm on the way. This nigga was crazy, but just because I was intrigued, I decided to go. Wrapping his plate up, I ran into Ty's room.

"I'm going right downstairs, do not leave out this door do you hear me?"

"Yes, mommy." Kissing him, I grabbed the food and headed down. I appreciated the fact that he parked facing my door, so that I could look out for Ty. Climbing in the car, I gave him the food and fork. He dug in, and didn't say a word until he was done.

"Where is my soda?" Passing him the can, I rolled my eyes in disbelief. "That shit was fye, you don't even look like you could cook. Your son good up there?" Nodding my head, I waited for him to begin. Taking a deep breath, he spoke again.

81

"My parents were killed on Christmas Eve, and me and Meek found them on Christmas day. I was fifteen, and I haven't gotten over the shit. When I sat in your place, the tree and decorations was getting to me. I had to get the fuck out of there."

"That's why Meek threatened to fire me if I brought any in the office." He nodded his head, and I felt bad for him.

"He wasn't as close to them, but me. My parents were my world outside of Meek. Some nigga felt that robbing someone for Christmas presents wasn't enough. They had to kill them. Why the fuck did they have to kill them?" Tears started to fall down his face. Knowing how he felt, I tried to reach out and comfort him.

"Fuck you don't touch me. Get out of my car. GET OUT!!!" This nigga checked out on me, and I wanted nothing more than to get the hell away from him. Slamming his door, I ran upstairs. Not just because he hurt my feelings, but his old hurt poured salt on my open wounds. Not even trying to put dinner up, I bathed Ty and put him to bed. The moment I was done, I showered and called it a night. Modest was stressing me, and he wasn't even

my nigga. I didn't like how he was able to control my emotions.
Fuck Modest, and everything he stood for.

****

"I haven't talked about this to anyone since it happened.
This is my first time even admitting how I feel to anyone. My
brother has been trying to get me to talk about it for years." This
nigga had broken into my house, and scared the shit out of me.

"How the fuck did you get in here? What are you doing
here?"

"You really should learn to lock your doors. Let me get this
out while I have the nerves. Seeing what you are going through, I
decided to tell you my story for you to see that you aren't the only
one having it bad during the holidays. Even though our situations
are different, we are hurting just the same.

It wasn't right for me to talk to you and treat you like I
have. For that I'm sorry. I don't know why I want to help you, but
I do. I'm not gone tell you that I will change being me, but I will
say that I will try to do better. It will be hard for me to come in
your place, hell its hard for me to drive around the city. This shit

eats at me everyday until the holidays are over. Those tears I shed earlier, was the first time I have cried since the funeral. I don't like the emotions you make me feel, just know when I go off, that's the place it's coming from. I'm sorry in advance." Not knowing what else to do, I wrapped my arms around him.

"We're more alike than you think. My baby's father was killed one week before Christmas last year. I have to live with that pain every day. Every single day since he has been gone, I have struggled. He was all I knew, and now I have nothing. I didn't even know where my next meal was coming from, until you showed up. You gave me more than you could ever know. The life you live, I know we can't be together. Don't get me wrong, I'm attracted to your rude, ignorant ass. I told myself after my baby's father, I would never date another street guy again."

This nigga pushed my gown up, and climbed on top of me. Everything in me was telling his ass to get up, but my pussy was on fire saying enter me.

"I'm not a street nigga. I'm co-owner of Matthews Realty. Now shut the fuck up and give me this pussy." Before I could protest, he had slid his fingers up and down my slit. The shit felt so good, I didn't want him to stop. It's been so long since someone touched me there, my juices were pouring out like crazy.

"I don't have a condom." Reaching in his pocket, he pulled one out. "You just knew you was gone hit huh?"

"Naw, I end up fucking in the most random places. These bitches be wild." Opening my mouth to tell him to get the fuck off me, he covered my lips with his. His tongue tasted sweet, and I knew I would crave it from this day forward. When his dick replaced his hand, I almost backed out. He felt so big against my small opening.

"Let me in." His voice was low, but demanding. Without thinking twice, I spread my legs slightly. "Let me the fuck in." Opening them completely, he slid inside, and I had to fight a tear from falling. Stroking me slow and deliberate, our bodies was in sync.

"Fuck. I knew your shit was tight as fuck." Pushing my legs back, he used them as leverage to go deep like he wanted. It was almost bearable until he picked up the pace. Trying my best not to scream out, I grabbed the pillow and muffled my cries.

"Don't fight it Malae, let me in." How far did this nigga wanna go? The tip of his dick was in my throat.

"You're in as far as it can go." Smacking my ass hard, I cried out. "Fuck Modest."

"You know what the fuck I'm talking about. Let me the fuck in Malae." Did this nigga mean my heart? Knowing he couldn't mean that, I turned my grown woman on and started throwing that shit back. My juices were flowing down my leg, and I wanted more.

"Fuck baby, I'm about to cum." Not wanting to miss that train, I matched his strokes trying to hurry up and get mine. Our bodies shook together, and we came in unison.

"Where the fuck you been the past nine Christmases?" Smiling, I fell asleep.

CHAPTER 11 MEEK

This girl Akina was every fucking thing, and I had to let her go. Knowing it was about to be a shit storm when I get home, I decided to enjoy my night out. We were laid up watching movies, and talking since I left the office. She was a breath of fresh air.

If it hadn't been for her breakdown earlier, I would have never known what she was going through. It took a strong person to pick up and try to keep pushing after you lose a kid. That was the reason I didn't want one until I was out of the street life. Niggas used that type of shit against you, and I would never give someone that much power.

I know the type of guilt she was carrying. I've had it with me for ten years. No one knew, not even Modest. Not only was I the one that brought in all of the presents, I was the last one in the house. Which means, I was the one that left the door open. I've had so many what if moments, the shit killed me on the inside. That's the reason she can't get passed Gabbie. In her mind, if she had got up when she called her, then she could have saved her life. It took a lot of prayer for me to get past my guilt. Knowing I had to be there for my brother, I couldn't wallow in that shit and let it break me down. When the last movie went off, my dick was so hard I knew I had to get out of here. Not ready to leave her just yet, I decided on something different.

"Let's go out to eat." She looked at me crazy.

"It's late and I would have to change. Can I get a rain check?"

"Not a chance in hell. You're perfect just the way you are. Trust me, I'm tired of seeing that shit. Now, you got five minutes to get the fuck up and follow me out the door, or I'm going to carry your ass out." She stood there looking at me in a daring stare. Snatching her up, her ass didn't have time to respond she was over my shoulder so fast.

"Put me down Meek." Walking her out the door, I made sure I bumped her head on the way out. "Ouch, that shit hurt." Laughing, I threw her in the truck and drove off. Heading to the Cheesecake Factory, I wanted to take her somewhere we could get a good meal, and she could be dressed down. Once our food was ordered, I turned to face her.

"I want to fuck you so bad. You just don't know how I want to bend you over this table, and slide my dick in and out of that tight ass pussy. If I wanted to fuck you Akina, would you let me?" The look of shock on her face was funny. Even though I wouldn't cheat on Vikki, I wanted her to know that was the only reason I wasn't already in her guts.

"You're married. We can't, I'm not that girl."

"That's not what I asked you." When she didn't respond, I stood up and walked to her side of the booth. "I asked would you let me fuck you." When she still didn't respond, I pushed her back against the seat. Thankful it was empty on our side, I ran my fingers between her legs. Hearing her moan was driving me crazy. "Tell me."

Her ass was playing hard to get, and I loved a fucking challenge. Smirking, I leaned down and took her clit in my mouth through her pants. Sucking until I know she felt it, her body started to shake. Getting up, I walked back to my side of the table and sat down. It took everything in me not to take her ass back to her place. She was blushing when the waiter walked up with our drinks.

"Why are you making this hard?" Lust was all over her face, and I wish I could give her what she wanted.

"You're the one making it hard. My shit been on brick since you walked in my office. My common sense is telling me I need to stay away from you, but I can't bring myself to do it. I'm drawn to you, and I have never wanted someone so bad in my life. There isn't a woman out there that made me want to cheat on my wife. She's a fucked up person, and I told you how we been at odds, but I still took a vow."

"You have to let me go Meek. It's not fair to me, or you for that matter. If I was your wife, I wouldn't want you out here spending the entire day with another woman."

"If you were my wife, I wouldn't have to." You could see the sadness in her eyes. We both mirrored the same what ifs. Me and Vikki had history, at one point, I thought she was it. After what we been through since I told her I wanted to go legit, and how she changed on a nigga, I wasn't so sure anymore. Being with

Akina all day, it felt like I have known her my entire life. We were

in sync on all levels, and it saddened me to know I couldn't have

all of her.

"Akina I want you to hear me, and hear me clear. I will

never let you go. No I can't have you, but you are mine."

"You sound crazy as hell right now. You been reading

about that nigga Phantom too?" Not knowing what the fuck she

was talking about, I was lost.

"What?"

"Never mind, but that is not fair. I deserve to have all of

someone, all of their heart. You can't give me that."

"The only thing I can't give you is sex. Are you telling me

you don't want to see me anymore?"

"I think it's best." Pissed, I tried to choose my words

carefully. Before I could respond, my phone rung.

"Come by the warehouse, we have a problem."

"On the way." Hanging up with Modest, I was glad our

food had arrived.

"Box this up for us, we have to leave." The waiter did as she was asked, and we got out of there. I hated the conversation ended on a fucked up note, but now my mind was on my money. Knowing I didn't have time to swing her home, I took her with me. When we pulled up, I got out.

"Stay here." Heading inside, Modest and Lando had this nigga named Green tied up.

"What's going on?" Green started yelling.

"I don't know what the fuck is wrong with these niggas. I'll never steal from you." Taking off my suit jacket, I reached for the pistol Modest had in his hand.

"First of all, watch your fucking tone when you're talking to me. Secondly, was my money short?"

"Yes, but." *Whack, whack, whack.* Never giving him a chance to finish his statement, I beat him with the gun until I was tired. What scared me was it had nothing to do with him or my money being short. I was still pissed Akina was going to let me see her after tonight. Somebody had to pay for the hurt I was feeling, may as well be the nigga that thought it was okay to take from me.

I knew I had to blank out, because Modest was looking at me crazy. It's been a long time since I did a nigga like this. Ignoring their looks, I continued my assault.

"Where the fuck is my money? I'm not for the bullshit, and you can save the lies. Choose to live nigga."

"I swear I don't know. The money was there, I counted it myself. Now all of a sudden, they saying it's short. Have I ever stolen from you?"

"The thing is, you're asking me to take your word over the only nigga I trust. No nigga will ever accuse my brother of anything, and live to tell it. Modest, you know what to do." Walking out, put my jacket back on and got in the truck.

"It's blood all over your shirt." Looking down, the shit was everywhere.

"He can thank you for that." We drove the rest of the way in silence. I was in my feelings, and I didn't like that shit one bit. Not wanting to prolong this shit any longer, when I dropped her off, I kept going. This shit was about to blow me because I knew my night was not over. Heading home, I prepared myself for the

fight I knew I was about to have with Vikki.

As soon as I got in the door, a heel went flying past my

face.

"Nigga you got me fucked up. Where the fuck have you

been?" Even though I knew I was dead to the wrong, I was not in

the mood.

"Vikki, it's been a rough day. I just want to lay down. We

will talk tomorrow."

"We gone talk tonight." She charged at me full force.

Timing it perfectly, I slid to the side right before impact. It took

everything in me not to bust my shit from laughing. She ran into

that wall so hard, that head had a hill on it.

"WHO THE FUCK IS SHE? Tell me Meek." Finally

looking at Vikki feeling bad, I noticed something. Her shirt was

inside out. Now to some people, this could have been an honest

mistake. That's if they didn't know Vikki. Amused, I looked over

the rest of her. Even though her hair was still in it's style, the back

was smashed in, and I couldn't be sure, but it looked like a slight

94

hickey on her neck. This bitch was cheating on me. ME! Meek

mother fucking Matthews. Damn near laughing out loud, I finally

responded.

"She is someone who respected you enough not to give me

the pussy. Get the fuck out of my face Victoria before I forget you

are my wife." Walking out the door. I had to get out of there, I

needed some air. A nigga was lusting over Akina all day, but I

didn't take it there because of my marriage. Yet, this mother fucker

out here just giving my pussy away.

Getting in my car, I drove with no destination in mind. We

been going separate ways for a while now, but I was willing to

work it out. Vikki had been apart of my life for as long as I could

remember, and I couldn't imagine her not being there until Akina

walked in my office. The time we spent together showed me how

unhappy I have been. Me and Vikki want different things, but I

love her ass.

This snake ass bitch was really out here bugging because I

went legit. I got a trick for her ass though. Once all my ducks were

in a row, I was leaving her behind when the New Year hit as well.

One thing I didn't tolerate was a snake, and I damn sure didn't lie down with them. Driving to the one place I knew I shouldn't be, I headed back to Akina's house. Hoping she hadn't fallen asleep, I knocked on her door. When it swung open, you could tell she had been crying.

"I just wanna be near you." Moving out the way, she let me in.

CHAPTER 12 MODEST

Heading to the strip club I was three fifty hot. This nigga Lando had me fucked up. His ass did the rounds today, but instead of turning in the money, his ass ain't been seen. No matter what goes on, I know this nigga would always come here at the end of the night. Pulling into the parking lot, the first car I see is his shit.

Grabbing my heat, I headed into the club ready to give this nigga a fade. This clown ass nigga was sitting at the stage throwing money, and the duffle bag sat next to him. Not even alerting him of my presence, I walked over and rocked that nigga to sleep. While the nigga twitched, I grabbed the money and threw it in my trunk. Heading back in the club, I waited for this trick ass nigga to wake up. He searched the club trying to figure out what happened. When his eyes landed on mine, he was looking at death.

"You thought it was okay for you to take our money and give it to these bitches?"

"I ain't gave them shit. I just didn't want to be counting the shit all night."

"Do it look like I give a fuck what you didn't want to do? You brought two hundred thousand into a strip club, while you sat here getting hard over a bitch that look like she got a baby penis."

"Gone head on, I wasn't looking at that bitch. She just came on stage. You know I don't rock like that, and it's not a dick, she just got an extremely big clit." Laughing, I grabbed the nigga and slammed him on the stage. Security looked like they wanted to step to us, but they knew who the fuck I was.

"Nigga you turned on by a fucking hermaphrodite. This bitch got a baby dick, you like dick nigga? Yeah I think you like dick." Lando was trying his best to get up, but he knew he couldn't fuck with me. Motioning for the girl on stage to come to me, she walked her saggy clit ass over like she was the shit.

"I'll pay you five hundred dollars to put your dick in his mouth." She had the nerve to get mad.

"I'm all woman you got me fucked up." Pulling my gun on her, this bitch was about to catch one.

"Look mister, your dick is long, your dick is strong, put the shit in his mouth or your ass is gone." She went to climb on top of him.

"Come on Modest, don't do this shit. You gone have niggas thinking I'm gay." Lando was in denial.

"Nigga they gay with you. All you nasty mother fuckers was in here throwing your money at mister while she shook her dick in your faces. What you do on your time is your business, but you decided to use our money." Looking over at mister, I got pissed. "Why the fuck are you still standing there? What did I ask you to do?"

She climbed on his face, and the nigga fought it all of thirty seconds. He must have been wanting her for a minute, because the nigga didn't even try to play it off. He was sucking on that shit like his life depended on it. Pulling out my phone, I recorded the nigga. Tears fell from my eyes I was laughing so hard. Now I see what chicks go through when they be trying to suck a lil dick. That mother fucker kept falling and sliding out. He was struggling to keep it in, but that didn't stop the nigga from trying. I was about to put my phone up when mister nutted on his face. The shit shot out everywhere. Now I don't know if the bitch nutted like us, or if she squirted. Either way, it looked like mister nutted on his ass. Putting my phone up, I got up to walk out.

"Hey where my money?" She actually thought I was gone pay for that nasty ass shit.

"The fairy got you." Laughing, I walked out and headed straight to Meek's house. This was Lando's last straw, his ass had to go. Not only did he jeopardize our money, but Meek did not do fairy's. Laughing my ass off, I knocked on his door. Vikki answered looking a hot mess. She stood there blocking the door.

"If you don't get your Susan B Anthony looking ass out the way. Fuck is wrong with you?" Her ass still stood there.

"He not here." Knowing why she was mad, I made sure to laugh in her face.

"Oh, he tipped and dipped. Fix your shirt, you got that shit inside out." When she looked down, fear crossed her face. Not giving a fuck what that shit was about, I jumped in my whip and headed to Malae's house. Lando could wait until tomorrow, right now, I needed some pussy. When I got to her crib I texted her. Not

wanting to seem like a creep just showing up.

Me: You up

HER: Yes.

Me: You coming down?

HER: No, Ty is woke, and we are finishing a project.

You coming up? Knowing she had all that Christmas shit up, I

really didn't want to, but I wanted to see her. Pushing my feelings

to the side, I got out and opened the door. Shaking my head

because it was open, I went off.

"Why the fuck is your door open?" Even though she threw

me a death look, she was looking sexy as fuck in her tight ass

gown.

"Don't talk like that in front of him. Ty this is Modest my

friend, and Modest this is my son."

"That's the mean man from the gas station." Laughing, I

hated that he remembered that shit.

"My bad lil man, I was having a bad day. What you

working on?"

"It supposed to be a reindeer, but mommy made a puppy." Laughing, her ass was fucking this baby project up.

"Malae, get me some more stuff, me and lil man about to do this over. You done made this rabid ass dog."

"We don't have anymore stuff. He needs to be sleep, it's just gone have to do." It was cute to see her think she was in charge.

"Go to Walmart, and get him some more stuff. You not sending my lil nigga to school with this sick ass dog." You could see the tears welling up in her eyes. What the fuck did I say wrong now? She leaned towards me trying to whisper.

"I need my gas, and you know I don't have it. He can use this." Shaking my head, I reached in my pocket and gave her a hundred dollar bill.

"Take my car and bring all the shit he needs, not that cheap shit either. We want snow, antlers, the nose, all that shit." Smiling she headed to the room to change her clothes.

Once she was gone, I talked shit "Don't worry lil man, I ain't gone let her send you off. Throw that uglass thing in the garbage before it bites us." You could tell he was nervous, but happy at the same time.

"You like our tree? I can't wait until Christmas Santa is gone bring me lots of toys. Look come here." Before I could think of an excuse, he grabbed me by my hand and pulled me towards the tree. Fighting back tears, I stood there while he showed me how Santa was going to get in and where he was going to leave the presents. Even though I wanted to be sad, and get the fuck away from the tree and decorations. His excitement was starting to rub off on me.

"Look, my parents always told me that you have to leave him cookies if you want good presents."

"You gone help me make the cookies? I really want a lot of presents. Mommy told me I had to be good, I been extra good all year." Knowing I really didn't want to do holiday shit, I knew I couldn't turn him down.

"Yeah I'll help you lil man. Did you already make your list?"

"No, my daddy usually helps me. He gone with the wings." Trying not to laugh, it was my turn to grab his hand.

"Come on, let's make you a list. How Santa gone know what to bring if you don't send him the letter?" The excitement that shot over his face had me saying fuck my feelings. Knowing what Christmas was to me before my parents died, I think all kids should experience that. Not to mention, if I was gone buy lil man's gifts, I would need to know what he wanted.

Of course, he felt we should sit by the tree and write it. It was crazy that this lil boy was able to do what so many others had failed at. He was helping me face my fears without having a clue as to what he was doing. Against my will, he made me write out my own list.

"What are you all doing?" Malae was looking shocked, but you could see the worry on her face. Nodding, I let her know I was good. Folding the papers up, I promised to take Ty to the mailbox tomorrow, so we could mail them.

ON THE 12TH DAY OF CHRISTMAS   LATOYA NICOLE

"We made our Christmas lists mommy. You have to do yours, but you have to hurry. Modest is taking us to mail them tomorrow."

"She can do her list while we do the project. Come on, it's late and we still have a reindeer to make." Malae was standing there damn near in tears, and I was ready to put her ass out. Every time you looked up, her ass was crying and shit.

We finally finished the project, and I was happy as hell. Lil man talked my ass to death. Heading in Malae's room, if I was going to do this Christmas thing, I only had one request.

"Baby, I promised Ty I would make cookies and shit with him for Santa. If I do this Christmas thing with yall, it has to be at my place. I'm not comfortable being in the hood. Not because I think I'm better, but because of what happened."

"I'm good with that, but you know we gone have to decorate your house right?" Sighing, I knew but I hoped I was ready.

"Cool, now give me some pussy."

CHAPTER 13 VIKKI

It's been over a fucking week and this nigga has not been home. At first, I was scared for that nigga to come back. When Modest mentioned my shirt being inside out, panic set in. Did Meek notice it? Was that why he left? A bitch was scared out of her mind, but then my crazy activated. He had me fucked up. This nigga had no proof that I did anything, nor did he even approach me about it. Even if he thought I had fucked up, this was not the way he was supposed to do it.

Not to mention, this nigga went on spree firing mother fuckers left and right. My side nigga needed this job in order for our plan to work, but his ass was at home looking stupid. Getting my shit together, it was time for me to put my big girl draws on and go get my man. Whoever the bitch was, had another thing coming if she thought she would fuck this up for me.

Looking over myself in the mirror, I made sure not a hair was out of place. Satisfied that I looked confident, and like new money, I headed to the office. As soon as I pulled up, my nerves were all over the place. Game time bitch. Switching as if I was trying to break my hips, I walked in the office like I owned that mother fucker. The girl that worked there wasn't at her desk, and my anger rose immediately. She walked out of Meek's office, laughing away. He was real friendly all of a sudden with this bitch.

"Bae stop, I have to do some work." When those words left her mouth, she didn't get a chance to see me. Punching her with all the hate in the world, that hoe head snapped back like she had whip lash. She was gone learn who the fuck Vikki was. Getting too cocky, I didn't follow up and the bitch bounced back like vinegar laced pussy.

"You tried the right mother fucker today bitch." Next thing I know, this bitch had me on the ground punching me in my throat. If a hoe could talk, I would have asked her ass, who the fuck punches somebody in the damn throat. This was the one time I wish I hadn't had on these damn heels, she was able to get me to the floor because of them. Seeing Modest pull her from me, I was happy as hell.

ON THE 12TH DAY OF CHRISTMAS

ON THE 12TH DAY OF CHRISTMAS

"Bae what the fuck are you doing?" Bae? Oh fuck, I done got this damn ass whooping for nothing. She fucking with him, not Meek.

"This bitch just fucking hit me. She got the right one, I'll stomp the shit out of this bitch." Modest was laughing at me as I stood up, dusting myself off.

"Slow down tiger, you can't be in here stomping the usher from church. God is not pleased. Vikki get your dumb ass on, Meek ain't here."

"Fuck you Modest. Tell your brother if he doesn't come talk to me, he is going to regret it." This nigga let her go as if he was telling her to beat my ass, and I was nobody's fool. Skipping my ass out the door, I got the fuck out of dodge. That bitch fight like she was a big bitch, and somebody took her lunch money.

Having no idea where this nigga was, or who he was with, I felt defeated. Not knowing what else to do, I went back to the house. When I walked in the door, I was hoping he had come home. Grabbing my phone, I sent him a text.

Me: If you don't want me to run my mouth, you better be here in the next thirty minutes. Don't fuck with me, you know I'm crazy. Get here!!! Hoping this would work, I ran upstairs and put on some sexy lingerie. Making sure I looked good, I went to the kitchen and started dinner. Hearing the garage go up, I smiled. He was still a smart man, and knew not to fuck with me. when he came through the door, I turned to greet him. Not expecting for him to snatch me up by my neck, for the second time today, my ass couldn't breathe.

"You know who the fuck I am. Don't ever in your fucking life threaten me. You won't live to tell that shit." When he released my neck, I damn near cried I was so happy.

"Why are you doing this to us? Don't you love me anymore?" He looked at me in disgust, and for some odd reason, it hurt.

"YOU DID THIS!!!" He rubbed his hand down his face, and I could tell it was bothering him as well. "Vikki, you did this. All I have ever asked was that you hold me down. All the spending, and crazy shit, that stiff ass bun in your hair. I've never complained, I let you do what you wanted. All I asked is that you be my wife. The minute a nigga wanted better for his self, you changed on me. Treating me like I'm some square ass nigga. You did the one thing no female should do to their nigga. You stopped believing baby." I don't know if it was the feeling that I was losing, or me losing Meek, but the tears fell from my eyes.

"I'm sorry baby. We can fix this, just give me the chance. All we have to do is focus, and work on us. As long as you still love me, we can fix this." Walking over to me, he wrapped his arms around me. Kissing me on my forehead, he leaned towards my ear.

"Not when you fucking another nigga. Now get the fuck out of my face." His bitch ass pushed me so hard, I damn near did a split to keep from falling. After all that, now I was pissed.

"You been gone for over a week, don't try to play innocent nigga. You're the one out here cheating. Don't try and turn this shit on me."

"That's where you're wrong. As bad as I want to fuck her, I honor my vows and I won't do that to someone. It won't be fair to her. I'm not even sure if we are done, but I do know I'm done trying. I love you Vikki, but you are a fucked up person. Get your shit together."

"Who is she Meek?" Walking past me, he went out the door and just like that, he was gone. Reality and panic started to set in at the same time. There was no way my side nigga could be fired, and me dumped. With my name not being on anything, I would have nothing. There was no way in hell I could go back to being that bitch. Something was gone have to shake, and I knew just what to do.

The Matthew brothers were about to feel my wrath, and it was time to get this show on the road. Fuck them.

CHAPTER 14 AKINA

Meek has been with me for the past two weeks, and even though I was loving it, the shit was torture. He was not home with that bitch, but she still had a hold on him. It was as if he was using me to piss her off, or he was just here to clear his head. Either way, the shit was frustrating.

Lying next to him feeling his body against mine, his smell, even the way he breathed in his sleep turned me on. No matter what though, he would not have sex with me. The most he would do is kiss me, and even then, you could see the guilt on his face. This was why I could never be someone's mistress, or side bitch.

The shit was mentally draining, and I was over this shit. Meek was gone have to make a choice, and do it soon. His ass ran out of here because of a text she sent him. Knowing we hadn't made anything official, he wasn't my man. There was no way I could tell him I didn't want him to go. Snatching my dildo out of my drawer, I headed to the bath I had ran. Fuck him. They could be together.

I was doing just fine without his ass, and I would be that when he is gone. If I wanted to be truthful to myself, I would admit that he helped keep my mind off Gabbie. I hadn't had a breakdown since he has been in my life. It's not like we don't discuss her or anything, but he has been helping me deal with it.

Forcing me to go to her grave, we sit out there for hours and just talk to her. Before we go, he says a prayer. No matter what, I will always be grateful to him. I'm just not about to play this back and forth with him and his bitch. Whenever he decides to come back, I'm going to get my key.

Sinking my body into the water, I kicked my legs over the side and slid my toy inside me. Mmmm fuck. Until Meek, I hadn't thought about sex. After the scene in The Cheesecake Factory, I ran and got one the next day. I wasn't about to play with his ass. How the fuck am I hurting myself? This shit hurt like all hell going in, but I was determined to get this nut. Pulling the tip back out, I rubbed it against my clit.

I smelled him before I felt him. His hand was rubbing my clit before I could even open my eyes. Not knowing if it was a dream, I kept them shut. If I opened them bitches, the shit might be a dream. When his finger slid inside of me, I arched my back so he could insert it further. Right as I was about to cum, his ass pulled it out.

"Please don't stop." He never responded, and when I opened my eyes no one was there. Damn, that was one hell of a dream. Fuck. About to finish myself off, he came back in naked. His body looked like it was sculpted by God himself. Walking over to the tub, in one swift motion, he grabbed me by my hair and pushed my mouth on his dick.

If I hadn't been fantasizing about this since I met him, a bitch may have been offended. Opening my mouth wide, I allowed him to have his way with my face. He was fucking it as if I didn't have a willing pussy. His dick got brick hard, and I just knew he was about to bust. Releasing my hair, he closed his eyes and I knew he was battling with his self.

"Turn around." Getting on my knees in the tub, I leaned against the wall. Feeling his dick slide against my clit, I almost came. His touch alone had me ready to orgasm.

"Are you sure this is what you want?" If this nigga don't put this dick in me, I'm gone slap his ass to sleep.

"Yes baby, please fuck me." There was more silence, and then he slammed that shit in me so hard I had to look for something to hold. It was an urgency in the way that he was fucking me. Like he needed me. The water, and his balls slapping against my ass was turning me on.

I've never had a nigga with a curve before, and it was like it was finding spots I didn't know I had. Staying on one spot, my body started shaking and I couldn't control it. I wasn't sure if I was having a seizure or not, until I creamed all over his dick. The moment I released, his pumps got more violent. They were so strong and aggressive, they snatched another nut out of me without warning.

"Akina I'm sorry baby." He was slapping me on my ass, and each pump was harder than the last. He apologized each time. "I'm so sorry baby. Please forgive me." Screaming out, another orgasm had found it's way out of my pussy. On cue, his body started shaking with mine. Feeling him snatch out, I knew he had

115

just released as well. Lying his head on my back, he apologized again.

"What are you sorry for Meek?"

"Because you should have left this beast asleep. Now I'm about to kill this pussy. After tonight, you won't be able to walk let alone leave me. Get the fuck out of the tub and climb on the dresser." Knowing I should be scared, my pussy meowed, and I slid my happy ass all the way in the room. In my mind, I was screaming yaassss beat this pussy up then. That was until he did just that. He fucked me hard and rough all night, and a bitch could barely sit down to piss.

CHAPTER 15 MEEK

As much as I wanted Akina, I was feeling fucked up. I was a nigga that took his vows seriously, and even though Vikki had fucked up, I didn't want to be that person. People have a prejudgment against street niggas. They think all of us are out here cheating, and fucking bitches left and right. That wasn't who I was, or ever wanted to be.

Knowing I wouldn't be able to think with Akina sexy ass here, I knew I had to go home and figure out what me and Vikki was doing. That's the reason I was trying not to have sex with her. I knew it would complicate things, and now no matter what I did, someone would be hurt.

A nigga had been doing good, but when I walked in there and saw her playing in that pussy, I couldn't take it. Praying she backed out, I was selfish enough to put the ball in her court. That was my first and last mistake. That pussy was so good, I don't know how I could ever walk away from her. Even though that pussy is fye, Vikki got the best head in the world. They was making this shit hard, and I didn't know what the fuck to do. On top of my female problems, I had to let niggas of my crew go before the holidays. I didn't want to do that, because a desperate nigga will do anything. Me and Modest was convinced that's what happened the night with my parents.

How the fuck stupid could Lando be. Nigga you did your rounds and took my shit to the strip club. Had I not gotten my money back, that nigga would be in that heavenly choir. Even though I only had a couple of weeks left, that type of stupidity was not accepted. On any level. The video was the icing on the cake.

Man when Modest showed me that shit, I almost passed the fuck out. Something was wrong with my brother. Who would think to do some sick nasty as shit like that, is what I was thinking. Until I saw the nigga was liking it. I'm sorry, that is some gay shit. Her clit was bigger than some niggas out here. What man that isn't gay, would be comfortable sucking on that thang?

Even though he was loving that shit, Modest ain't have to do him like that in front of the entire damn club. Shit was getting hectic, and I knew that it was about to get worse. Looking over at

118

Akina sleeping, I tried to be fully dressed before I let her know that I had to go home. My ass hasn't even been to the office. Knowing that was the first place Vikki would look, Modest took over for me giving me a break. Him and Malae were growing close and I was happy as hell. My brother needed this, and even if they didn't work out, this would be the first Christmas he wasn't sad.

"Baby where are you going?" Fuck. Knowing I had to be honest, I faced her with regret in my eyes.

"I can't keep hiding out here. Me and Vikki need to figure out what we are doing, or it's only going to end up worse. Please don't be upset with me, I just need to get my head straight." Jumping off the bed, she slapped slob from my mouth.

"Fuck you Meek. Get the fuck out of my house. You are a coward and you used me. Just leave. Please." Not wanting to hurt her anymore, I grabbed my keys and left. That was the last thing I wanted to do, but it had to be done. When she calms down, I believe that she will understand what I needed to do. This was not the way to do this, and I would be less of a man if I didn't do it right.

119

Pulling up to my house, I needed a suit to put on. Even though Modest was the other owner, his ass was more focused on Malae right now. I needed to make sure shit was good, and running smoothly. Vikki was lying on the couch, and this may be the first time I didn't see her in heels. She had on some joggers, and a tank. In Vikki's world, she looked bad. To me, she looked sexy as hell.

"You came to get the rest of your stuff?" Looking at her, I could tell she had been crying.

"Naw, I'm home. We need to figure out if we are staying, or walking away. That can't happen if I'm not here." You would think the bitch would be happy, run into my arms, or something. She smirked, and I was starting to think this was a mistake. Heading upstairs, I changed as fast as I could and got the fuck out of there. Vikki ain't even try to stop me. Her ass was on a call when I left.

Walking in the office, I almost passed out. Modest has been here every day, so I know he saw this shit. It was Christmas decorations put up. Not a lot, but they were here none the less.

"What's this?" She smiled, and it felt as if I could breathe.

120

"Progress." Knowing what she meant, I headed to the office. Modest was behind the desk working, and I was proud of him. At one point, he thought he wouldn't be able to do this. Scared was an understatement, but I had total faith in him. When he started school, he realized it was actually something he liked. More than a street savage, he aced that shit with flying colors. Not wanting to push him, I didn't mention the decorations.

"It's good to see your ass been working. What you working on?" Never looking up, I knew how others felt when I did it to them.

"This client is looking for something very specific. He doesn't want to build; his ass wants the shit already there. Nigga pissing me off because he got me looking for a house with a damn wine cellar. You know how hard it is to find that shit?" Laughing, it would be hard if I had not been looking at a house that had one. It was nice as hell, and I wanted to buy it. The first thing I said was it had to go.

"I know a house. Give me the list of everything he is looking for, and I will see if it matches up." The nigga was happy as hell, and threw me the file.

"I'm about to take Malae to lunch. We been working like dogs all morning." Nodding my head, I looked at the file. It was time to get to work.

After three hours, I had found the house he was looking for, but it wasn't under our company. It took me two more hours to convince the owner to allow us to represent him, instead of selling private. That was going to be one hell of a commission, but I was frustrated behind it all. When my door opened, I looked up hoping it was Modest. A nigga was ready to go home.

Seeing Vikki walk through the door in some jeans and Ugg boots, made my dick jump. It's been a long time since I saw this Vikki. She didn't realize how good she looked like this. Don't get me wrong, she was fine no matter what, but that stuffy shit was not sexy. Thinking she was ready to talk, I came around and sat on the edge of the desk. She dropped to her knees, and undid my pants.

"Vikki what are you doing?" Never answering, she had my dick in her hands in seconds. Knowing she had the best head out there, I didn't attempt to stop her. When her mouth covered my dick, guilt overcame me. Vikki was my wife, and I had no idea what me and Akina was, but the shit felt wrong. Trying to push her away, she deep throated me, and I was done.

Telling her we needed to figure out what we were doing, I knew she wasn't wrong. Fuck, and it felt good as shit. Even though my legs were shaking, and my knees was weak, I felt bad. Every time I would convince myself I needed to stop, she would do some kind of trick that brought my mind back in the room.

"Fuck baby, suck that shit." Her slurps were pushing me over the edge, and her tongue tracing my balls had me ready to nut all down her throat. "You gone catch it baby?" When Vikki got on her stuck up shit, she stopped swallowing. I'm sure she wasn't about to now, but it didn't hurt to ask.

She didn't respond, but her ass started going harder on my shit. Grabbing her head, I knew my nut was about to cum.

"Fuck baby, I'm about to cum." Letting her head go, I gripped the desk and held on for dear life. As soon as my seeds shot out, she swallowed them mother fuckers like they were a snack. Even though my dick was limp, she kept sucking and it felt like my shit was getting a massage. When she kissed the tip, I knew she was done and I opened my eyes. The shit was so good, I never realized someone else was in the room.

"Akina, baby let me explain." The tears were pouring down her face, and my heart broke.

"Don't bother." She took off running.

"Baby, what the fuck you mean baby?" Trying to hurry up and fix my clothes, I took off after her never even responding to Vikki. When I got outside, she was standing with her door open.

"Congratulations. You built me up, so you could tear me down. You're the worse kind of person. At first sight, you're a God send. You make a person feel like they should be thanking God for you every night. You laid up in my house every day making me fall for you. The moment I did, you left.

One day. You weren't gone one day, and this is where I found you. My heart was in a million pieces when I met you, you healed me only to shatter me to a point of no repair. Stay the fuck away from me."

"Bye bitch. That's what your ass gets fucking a married nigga?" Akina didn't even respond, she jumped in her car and drove off. It wasn't until the tears found their way down my face, that I realized I didn't want to be here. "You crying over a bitch Meek?"

"Vikki we are done. I can't do this anymore. You can keep the house until you find out what you are going to do. I'll stay with Modest. I'll have a lawyer draw up some papers."

"Are you kidding me? Your side bitch of a couple of weeks curse you out, and now you're crying and divorcing me. Nigga you're weak. Fuck you." Not even having the strength to fight with her, I walked back in the office. All these years with Vikki, I felt nothing when she just walked away. Akina left, and it feels like she snatched my soul and took it with her. What the fuck was I thinking. No longer willing to wait until Modest came back, I left the office and went straight to his house. The moment I stepped

inside, I cried for the first time in years. What the fuck was going

on? The first Christmas in ten years, it seemed my brother's life

was coming together. In the same breath, mine was falling apart.

Grabbing my phone, I dialed Akina. Since it was going

straight to voicemail, I knew she had blocked me. FUCK. I messed

this up bad, and I had to figure out a way to fix it before it got

worse.

CHAPTER 16 MALAE

Even though things were starting to look up for me, I had to be smart. Receiving my first paycheck, I paid my rent and gas bill. As bad as I wanted to buy Ty some presents, I was the adult. Always been one to put my priorities first, I would never put wants before needs.

Modest was getting better about Christmas, but I wouldn't dare ask him to buy Ty's presents. My next check came after, and I would buy him some stuff then. It wouldn't be all that he wanted, but at least he would have something. The greatest gift was seeing Ty and Modest bonding. As soon as he would walk in the door, Ty ass be all over him.

I had him pegged so wrong, he was nothing like I thought. Knowing I couldn't be with him if he was in the streets, I was happy to learn never to judge a book by its cover. Watching him at work turned me on, and while Meek was out, we fucked all up and through there.

Trying to get him used to the decorations, I eased them in one by one. He never said anything, and it seemed like it didn't bother him. Wanting to make sure he was all the way comfortable, we had yet to decorate his house. Today would be the day, and I was excited. He didn't seem to be nervous or anything, and he even went with me to get the stuff. Of course, he had to pay, but he didn't have to go.

Our ass should have been back to the office, but he wanted to walk around the mall and look at some stuff first. He was in Footlocker looking at boots, and I chose to sit my ass down. It seemed like we had been in every damn store.

"Malae, long time no see. How are you holding up?" Seeing Lando made my past flash before my eyes. Him and my baby daddy were close friends, and I hadn't seen him since the funeral. Running to him, I jumped in his arms.

"How have you been? You said fuck your lil sister and moved on with life." The girl with him was looking uncomfortable until I said sister.

"I've been good, and that ain't true. I just thought it would be hard for you to see me. Maybe I was wrong for that, and I'm sorry. Hit me up sometimes, maybe we can catch up and grab some food." Taking my phone out, we exchanged numbers. Jumping in his arms again, I hugged him goodbye. This time, I was snatched in the air.

Before I could tell Modest what was going on, he punched Lando so hard his body jerked and hit the ground. Shocked, I have no idea why he was this upset.

"Baby, that's my baby's father best friend. You just put him to sleep for nothing. What is wrong with you?" Lando's girlfriend was trying to wake him up, when the nigga started snoring, it took everything not to laugh.

"When the nigga wakes up, you can tell him not to use your number. I don't give a fuck who he is to you."

"Wake up? The way he jerked, he might be dead. Modest why the fuck would you do that?"

"Maybe the nigga will wake up dead. Listen I don't give a fuck about that nigga. Stay the fuck away from him, and I won't repeat myself." Lando started groaning, and I wanted to help him up, but the look in Modest's eyes, told me that wouldn't be smart.

"You stay snaking a nigga. You and your brother think yall got shit all figured out. Fuck you." Lando was pissed, and I didn't blame him. I wondered how they knew each other.

"Looks like you already getting fucked. You left your wife for mister huh. Or are you cheating with the lil dick bitch? Go suck something and get the fuck out of my face. You know me." Modest didn't say shit else, but the look he gave Lando scared me. Must have scared him too, because he walked off.

"That was a dude?" I was so lost on who had a dick.

"Naw, ol girl got a baby dick. She a stripper. Why you worried about her dick anyway? You into that kind of thing?" Laughing, I slapped him in the head.

"Fuck you. Come on, we have to go pick up Ty." Even though Modest laughed and joked all the way to his house, especially when Ty got in the car. His angry vein was still bulging, so I knew he was pretending. I know he told me not to meet up with Lando, but I had to know how they knew each other and why

Modest was so upset.

****

Even though I could tell something was bothering Meek, he

looked so sad. Whatever was going on, I was glad he was here to

witness this. He smiled harder than I did every time Modest put an

ornament on the tree. If it was bothering him, you couldn't tell.

This was a beautiful moment, and I was glad I was a part of it.

The music was playing, and everyone had a cup of hot

cocoa. Ty was all over the place. He was all over Meek and

Modest. The fact that they didn't seem to mind, had me feeling

good.

"I wanna say something." Modest had the floor, and I could

tell it was about to get serious. "Ten years ago, I felt like my world

had ended. Every year, Christmas reminded me of what I lost. It

was hard for me to feel anything for anybody because I was scared

of losing them. My brother tried his best to help me heal, but I was

a lost cause. Until my lil man begged me for some change in the

gas station." Everyone laughed, but he never smiled.

"No kid should ever have to experience that kind of hurt, and I carried that shit with me for years. Every tree, every light, every present only reminded me of what I lost. Until, I met Malae. Thank you for teaching me to look at what I gained, and not what I lost. You have given me more than you will ever know. Thank you all for everything." You could tell he was fighting back tears, but I was proud of him. He had come so far.

Him and Meek shared a hug, and I knew it was hard on both of them. Meek was just better at hiding his pain. Ty pushed his self between them, and forced them to hug him as well.

"Since so many Christmas miracles are taking place today, I think I'm going to leave and try my luck. I hope some of yall shit rubbed off on me." Meek grabbed his coat and I prayed it worked out for him.

"Okay Ty, it's time for bed. Go head to Modest's guest room and get washed up." He groaned, but he did what I asked when he saw the look Modest gave him.

After Ty was done, I jumped in the shower and handled my shit as well. Modest had already been in, and he was laying across the bed waiting on me. Trying to figure out why he looked so

perplexed, I didn't know what to say. Giving him time, I waited

until he was ready to speak.

"I want you to teach me how to eat your pussy." Not sure if

I heard him right, I almost fell off the bed. He had never gone

down on me, but I was so gone off the dick I didn't ask why.

"You don't know how?" Sitting up, he looked me dead in

the eye.

"I have never eaten pussy a day in my life. Never planned

on it, but your scent drives me crazy. It makes me want to know

what that mother fucker taste like. Can I taste it Malae?" I almost

jumped on his lip.

"You sure?" Snatching the towel from around me, he stared

at me again making me leak down my leg.

"Let me taste you Malae." Walking towards him, I kicked

my leg up on the bed. Sliding his tongue up my slit, his moans

made me shiver. "Mmmm. Now what?" It was almost funny that a

grown ass man hadn't ate pussy, but it turned me on as well

knowing no one else had that part of him.

"Suck on my clit gently." Covering my clit with his mouth, my knees got weak. He was so gentle, but aggressive at the same time. You could tell he was scared to do it wrong, but the aggressor in him kept taking over. "Fuck baby just like that." Hearing my moans made him cocky. Wrapping his arms through my legs, he scooped my ass in the air and stood up.

Slamming me against the wall, the pain that shot through my body, and the pleasure of his tongue was driving me crazy. Feeling my nut coming, I started grinding against his face. Slamming me against the wall again, I knew he wanted to be in charge. Flicking his tongue against my clit, he waited for my moan to make sure that he was doing it right. Going crazy, I was about to nut when he slammed me down on his dick.

"Nigga. What the fuck." Smiling, he didn't show any mercy.

"Shut up and take this dick." Between his dick banging my cervix, and my head hitting the wall, this nigga was fucking the shit out of me. All I could scream in my head was, help me. No one answered, because this nigga was tearing a lining out of my

ass and didn't give a shit about my kitty.

"Fuck me Malae." You would think he would slow up to let

me, but nope. He kept right on slamming his dick inside of me.

"FUCK ME MALAE."

"I'm trying." Taking me to the bed, he laid me down and

pushed my legs so far back, my ass flew in the air on its own.

Instead of sliding his dick back inside, he finger fucked me in the

ass.

"Fuck, wait. Modest baby hold on." Not listening, he

inserted two fingers. "FUCK BABY, GIVE ME A MINUTE.

FUUCKKK." You would think he had his dick inside me the way

he was fucking my ass with his fingers. With tears falling down

my face, all I could do was take it. Sliding his fingers out, he

wrapped his mouth around my clit again. My body shook violently,

and all I wanted to do was go the fuck to sleep.

Sliding his dick back in, all I could do at this point was

whimper. "Please baby." Taking his time. He slid in and out

slowly. With my pussy finally getting a break, I sighed from relief until his pace picked up again.

"Can I nut in you Malae?" Not knowing how to answer that, I didn't. "Can I nut in my pussy Malae?" When he picked the pace up, I knew my girl couldn't take another assault like that.

"Yes baby." Feeling his body shake, I had never been happier.

"Fuck, baby this shit coming whether you want it or not. Fuck." His seeds shot through me, and I was out before they hit my eggs. A bitch was tired.

CHAPTER 17 MEEK

Seeing my brother and Malae together, had me willing to put myself out there on the line. Hell, all kinds of Miracles happened at Christmas. Why the fuck I couldn't have one. It took me to fuck up, to realize where I wanted to be, but I know now.

Akina was in her feelings, but at the end of the day, Vikki was my wife and I needed to make sure I was making the right decision. Driving to her house, I drove through the city fast as hell. You would think she was about to leave town or some shit, and I was trying to catch her.

This shit was urgent than a mother fucker, and I needed her like I needed air. Pulling up to her place, I jumped out. Knocking on her door, I waited while I prayed she answered.

"Meek don't do this. Just leave me alone." Her ass didn't even open the door for a nigga, she yelled the shit.

"Just let me explain." Even though it was cold as fuck outside, she was worth it. "I didn't want to hurt anybody. When I made my decision, I wanted to make sure I was making the right one. You can't fault me for not wanting to act on impulse. You had been through enough, and Vikki was all I knew. All I knew was you felt right, and it wasn't fair to you. I'm sorry, but the moment you left, I knew you were the right one for me. You don't have to forgive me right away, all I'm asking is that you give us a chance to fix it." There was a silence, and I hoped she was still by the door.

"We had our chance, please just leave me alone." Leaning against the door, I wanted to kick that mother fucker in. Choosing not to, I had to honor her wishes. A nigga fucked up, and I had to accept it.

"I'm sorry Akina. One day I hope you can realize that. I told Vikki I wanted a divorce, and I'm staying at my brother's house. I'm not trying to force you into anything, I just wanted you to know that it's over with me and her."

"If you left her for me, then it wasn't the right reason. You have to make the decision for you. I'm hurt, but I want you to be happy even if it's with her."

"Akina, whether you come back or not, me and Vikki are done. Please just think about it. You know where to find me. Just know that everything we shared was real." When she didn't respond, I walked away. Not wanting to go back to the happy couple with bad news, I headed to the office. There was no way I was going to my house.

Getting out of the car, I was unlocking the door when the shot fired off. My body jerked, and before I could figure out what the fuck was going on, more shots rang out. My body was on fire, and I fought to keep my eyes open. Akina would never know I love her, and my brother will hate Christmas forever.

The only thing that went through my mind is I failed him. He was doing better, and no one or nothing will ever make him love this holiday again. It took him ten years to get over my parents, now he would lose his entire family the same way. Tears fell from my eyes, and I hated that I was so upset I didn't pay attention to my surroundings.

Funny thing is, they say when you lose one sense, you gain another. My eyes were closed, but I could hear Vikki. I knew the clacking of those heels anywhere. Fighting to open my eyes, they

stood over me and pulled the trigger. I never saw that shit coming,

and it was no way I could warn my brother. Closing my eyes one

last time, I prayed. Praying for my soul, and my brother's strength

I took my last breath.

CHAPTER 18 MODEST

Last night had a nigga feeling good. Eating pussy wasn't as bad as I thought. Even though the type of bitches I fucked, I probably wouldn't have eaten that shit no way. Her pussy tasted so good, I woke up in the middle of the night licking that mother fucker. That wasn't the only reason though.

I didn't give a fuck about the other chicks I was with, so I never put effort into fucking they ass. It wasn't that I didn't know how to fuck, I was actually a beast. Knowing how I liked to be in control of most shit, I knew I had to master eating pussy. She wasn't about to be telling the next mother fucker my head was just okay. The way she was moaning let a nigga know he was doing pretty good, I wanted to eat her shit so good that mother fucker left with me when I got up.

Smelling her scent in my beard, I jumped in the shower and washed my shit. Even though I loved that shit, I ain't want a mother fucker talking shit about me having pussy in my beard.

After I was done conditioning it, I got out and got dressed. Malae was trying to climb back in the bed fully dressed.

"Bring your ass on. You gotta go to work. Meek gone think you slacking cus you fucking the boss. I know you don't want people to think you fucked your way to the top, do you?" Groaning, she sat up.

"Fuck you Modest. I'm sleepy and my pussy hurts. It's your fault my shit feels like it's by my knees. I just need thirty more minutes."

"Get your ass up. We have to drop Ty off." When she finally got up, I decided to throw something at her. "Baby I was thinking. Since we with each other every day, why not make it official." Her ass started choking, and I had to shut her down. "You wish, I just learned how to eat pussy. I'm definitely not marrying a mother fucker. I mean us moving in together."

"I wouldn't marry you anyway asshole." Grabbing her, I kissed her soft ass lips. "Who told you to wash my pussy off your beard?"

"You tried it. Wish the fuck I would walk around with coochie crust in my shit. Now answer the question."

"I have to talk it over with Ty first, but if he is okay with it, yes."

"Well you may as well start packing, that's my lil man. He gone be with it."

"I'll have a talk with him after school. I'm going to drive my own car so that way me and him can talk alone."

"Cool, I'll see you at the office." Walking out the door, I was in a damn good mood and nothing could change that shit. For the first time in forever, I was happy about Christmas. I would start shopping soon, but I had to find a way to do it without them being around. We were always together. Meek was gone have to help me out with this shit.

Pulling up to the block that our office was on, I couldn't get up the street. It was police cars, and an ambulance blocking the shit off. Parking where I could, I got out and walked down. Malae's perfume was on me, and my dick was so hard I didn't feel the cold. The closer I got, for some reason an uneasy feeling came over me.

143

It almost felt like ten years ago. Shaking the shit off, I continued towards the door.

"Excuse me sir, this is a crime scene you can't go any further." Trying to see what was going on, it was impossible.

"What happened? I'm one of the owners of the Realty company right there." A look came over his face, and my nerves kicked in again.

"You're the other owner?"

"Yeah, what's going on?"

"Can you tell us who else works there?"

"You about to piss me the fuck off. What's going on?" Seeing that he wasn't gone respond until I answer, I told him. "Just me, my brother, and our receptionist."

"I'm sorry to inform you, but your brother was shot sometime tonight." He was here until the store owner next door came and found him." Not waiting to hear anything else, I took off running towards the ambulance. They were closing the door, and I tried to tear that mother fucker off.

"Sir, we have to go."

ON THE 12ᵀᴴ DAY OF CHRISTMAS

"That's my fucking brother. I need to see him."

"Listen, your brother was shot six times. If there is any hope of us saving his life, we have to go right now."

"Where are you taking him?"

"Cook County." Walking off, she jumped in and drove off. Trying to get back to my car, the officer stopped me.

"We need a statement from you." He must have lost his mind.

"If you don't get the fuck out of my face. I need to get to my brother. I wasn't here how the fuck am I going to give you a statement." Pushing past him, Malae was walking up.

"Baby what's going on." Not responding I kept walking. Grabbing me by my arm, she tried to pull me to her. "What's wrong Modest?"

"You are what's wrong. You came into my life and gave me this false hope that Christmas could be a holiday for me again. The shit was a fucking lie, and I'm over the shit. Get the fuck away from me so I can go check on my brother."

"What happened to Meek?"

"Are you fucking dumb? Leave me the fuck alone so I can go check on my brother. Go sing some fucking Christmas carols, and lie to another nigga about how the shit is a special day." When I got to my car, I peeled off. Knowing I was away from everyone, I pulled over. "Fuck. Fuck. Fuck. Fuuuckkk. God why now? Please don't take my brother. He is all I have left. What the fuck man. Please God, don't take the only person I have left." Leaning against the steering wheel, I cried.

This holiday just didn't like a nigga. Putting my car in drive, I headed towards the hospital. Even though I knew where I was going, I was lost. Who the fuck inflicts this kind of pain on one person? What did I do to deserve this type of hurt?" When I pulled up to the hospital, I was too scared to go in. Sitting there staring at nothing, I cried.

Finally getting up the nerve to go inside, it felt like the weight of the world was on my shoulders with every step. How could this happen? This shit felt like a bad dream, and I didn't know how to wake the fuck up. Walking up to the desk, I tried to find out some information.

"Excuse me, I'm trying to find out some information on my brother. He was just brought in." The bitch kept writing like I wasn't standing there. Snatching her folder, I hit her ass in the forehead with it. "Earth to inconsiderate bitch. I asked you a question, and it would be in your best interest to answer me." You could tell she wanted to go the fuck off, I'm sure the look in my eyes told the five foot dummy to be smart.

"What's your brother's name?" Her attitude was about to piss me the fuck off.

"Fix your tone, and that crunchy ass wig. I'm trying not to fuck you up because my brother is more important, but if you keep pushing me, we gone have a problem. His name is Meek Matthews, and he was just brought in within the last half hour." Typing in his info, she looked up at me with sadness in her eyes.

"He's in surgery. The doctors will come and talk to you when they can. I hope he makes it." Not caring about her concern, I walked off and sat down. God please don't do this to me. While I waited, I cried.

CHAPTER 19 MALAE

What in the entire fuck was going on? How did we go from having a great night, to straight disaster? All this work to get him past his parent's death, and then this happens. I couldn't even imagine what was going through his mind. I'm sure all the old pain came back, and is now mixed with what just happened to Meek. What I don't understand, is his attitude towards me.

It's like he was blaming me for taking his mind off the shit. He accused me of bullshitting him with smoke and mirrors, but all I was trying to do was help him heal. There is no way I could have guessed something like this would happen. Not even knowing exactly what happened to Meek, I got in my car and went to the hospital.

He may not know it now, but he needs someone. He needs me. Knowing this wasn't going to be easy, I took a deep breath and walked inside. His entire demeanor was breaking my heart. He looked so broken, and defeated. I had no idea what to say to him. I'm sure he didn't want me to say shit, so I just sat next to him.

Placing my arms around his shoulder, I held him as he cried. A doctor approached us, and my heart stopped I was so scared.

"Matthews family?" Modest nodded, and the doctor continued. "He was shot six times. Once in the back, twice in the side, Twice in the shoulder, and once in the chest. Someone wanted him dead, but he is a fighter. He coded a couple of times, but he is stable right now. His body went through a lot of trauma, and right now he is non responsive. I don't see any complications stopping him from making a recovery, right now it's all up to him. Any questions for me?" Modest didn't respond, so I nodded for him. When he left, I tried to talk to him.

"He's going to be okay, Meek won't leave you. This is a good thing, it could have been worse." His body started shaking, and I knew he was crying again. Hugging him, I just kept whispering in his ear. "It's going to be okay." His body calmed, and he turned to look at me.

"Get the fuck out. I don't want you here." Looking at him in disbelief, I tried to figure out what the fuck I did wrong.

"Excuse me?"

149

ON THE 12TH DAY OF CHRISTMAS   LATOYA NICOLE

"You got ten seconds to get the fuck out, or I will drag you out. Stay the fuck away from me." Not wanting to encounter any more embarrassment, I got up and left. He was hurting, so I didn't blame him for his reaction. I know he will come around, right now he just needs space to deal with it by himself.

This Christmas was slowly starting to go down the drain. For a minute, everything was perfect. Now nothing was certain, and I was trying to figure out a way to pick up the pieces. Needing something to do with my time, I went back to the office. Meek would be upset if he came home, and everything was out of order.

When I got back, the block was cleared out. It was a woman outside the door, and I was happy I decided to stop there. She looked cold, so I assumed she had been out here for a while.

"Excuse me, can I help you with something?" When she turned to me, I knew it was the girl from a few weeks ago. Tears filled her eyes, and I couldn't deal with anymore bad news.

"When he left my house, I was being stubborn. I guess the cocky side of me expected him to still be on the other side of the door. When I finally opened it, he was gone. Running after him, I tried to catch him, but I couldn't. I said to myself, a few more hours won't hurt him. I'll go to him in the morning. Knowing we were finally going to get our chance, I got up with a new purpose. My dumb ass smiled all the way here. Walking up, I saw all the blood. My soul is telling me something happened to him." She finally looked me in the eyes. "What happened to Meek?"

"He was shot six times last night. I just left the hospital, and he is stable. It's up to him at this point." She just kept nodding her head. "Would you like to come in?"

"No, I need to go see him. He needs to know how I feel, just in case." Wiping tears from her face, she gave me a weak smile. "I'm Akina, hopefully we can talk under better circumstances."

"I'm Malae. Go see about him, we will have plenty of time to talk. He's a fighter." Wondering if I should warn her about Modest, I thought better of it. I'm the one he was upset with. She should be fine.

After going stir crazy sitting in that office, I had to get the hell out of there. Grabbing all of my stuff, I headed out the door.

As soon as I got in my car, my phone went off. Assuming it was Modest, I didn't even look. I just answered.

"Hey, is everything okay?"

"Why wouldn't it be? I take it that nigga got you going through it again." Looking at the phone, I realized it was Lando.

"What are you talking about?"

"Can we meet somewhere. I think it's something you should know about your man." My mind was telling me to honor Modest's wishes, but my heart knew it was something I needed to know. After telling him to meet me at the office, I hung up.

Just the fact that somebody wanted Meek dead told me, there was a lot I didn't know about them. Modest promised me he wasn't in the streets, but I'm starting to wonder if that was a lie. Why would someone shoot Meek six times and not take anything? Question after question invaded my mind as I waited. Realizing I didn't give him the address, I grabbed my phone. Before I could dial his number, he was tapping on my window. Unlocking the door, he got in.

"Damn no hug?" Last time I hugged him, Modest came out of nowhere, and wreaked havoc. I was not about to try that shit again.

"Just talk Lando. What the hell is going on?" His expression changed, and I was now scared.

"Me and June worked for Meek and Modest. They been running the streets of the Chi for years. June stole some money from them because he didn't want you to know how bad you all were struggling. When they figured out it was him, it was a wrap."

"Are you telling me, they killed my baby's father?"

"I'm telling you, Modest killed him. Meek wasn't even there. I tried to talk him out of doing it, but he beat me with a gun, and I knew I couldn't cross them niggas or I would have the same fate. I sat there and watched my nigga die, and it wasn't shit I could do about it." Taking in everything he said, I couldn't do shit but cry. A bitch was so tired of crying, I didn't know what the fuck to do. Just when I thought this shit couldn't get any worse, it went bad.

"I need to go home. Thank you for telling me. Take care Lando." Climbing out of the car, he thought about it.

"Please don't tell him I told you." Nodding my head, he closed the door and he was gone.

All the way home, only one question crossed my mind. How the fuck did I fall for the nigga that tore my world apart?

CHAPTER 20 VIKKI

My plan was coming together, and nobody could tell me shit. Meek thought he was so fucking smart, but I'm that bitch. No nigga will leave me in the cold broke starving and gang banging. Who would do that shit to their wife any fucking way? Me and this nigga been together more than half of our lives, and he had no intentions on giving me a dime.

The minute he told me he was going legit, I knew the nigga was gone change up. We were one and the same, but I wasn't with that nine to five shit. The moment we started arguing about the shit, I knew I had to start coming up with a plan. This shit ain't just start, it just started to come together for me this year. Heading to my side nigga's house, I was elated at the shit we had done.

It turned me on to see that nigga lying there weak, and helpless. When he opened his eyes and saw me standing there, I knew it was then, in that moment, he knew he had fucked up. It took everything in me not to laugh. We didn't have time for that, we could gloat later. There was no way that nigga could make it

155

after all them hits to his body. Walking in the door, I screamed and jumped around like a kid.

"Oh my God baby, did you see his face?" Lando wasn't as happy as I was, and he was starting to piss me off.

"The plan was for him to be shot in the head. Why did you change it?" This nigga was tripping. My ass wasn't bout that life, and he lucky I did the chest shot. The only reason I did that, was to see the look on his face. I wanted him to know how he fucked up crossing me. I'm not a killer.

"He was hit six times, how the fuck can he survive that shit?"

"You know fifty cent was shot nine times, even got hit in the face." Was this nigga serious right now.

"You do know that nigga was lying right? It was a fucking movie. Grow up. Look at where he was hit. That nigga died in our face, there is no way he made it."

"You better be right, or I'm going to save my own ass. I'm not going out like June." Smacking him across his face, he had officially pissed me off.

"Don't forget I'm the mother fucker putting you on. If you follow my plan, you will be running the city. You try to fuck me, your ass gone end up just like June." As I said, this shit didn't just start. Me and June had been fucking around for a couple of years. He was everything I wanted in a nigga. Fine, big dick, and wanted to be the king of the streets forever.

I went to him, and showed him a sure way to take down Meek. We were robbing that nigga for a minute, but I was ready to move on with my plan. I was tired of pretending, and I wanted to be with my man. This nigga was gone over his lil bitch at home, and wouldn't leave. Feeling betrayed, I set the nigga up and had his ass killed.

Meek didn't want to be in the streets anymore, but the shit ran through his blood. Even though it was only five thousand dollars, I knew he wouldn't let that nigga off the hook. June never saw that shit coming. Lando wasn't really my type at first, but the plan had to go on. They treated that nigga like shit, and Modest beat his ass if he blinked wrong.

He was the perfect candidate, and now he standing here threatening me like he has forgotten who the fuck I am. Coming up with a plan after Lando got his dumb ass fired, was hard as hell. Modest was the key. If we broke him, we could get it all. We had been going at it the wrong way all this time.

Killing Meek, everything would go to Modest. The thing is, that nigga be in his feelings. He will not ever step foot back in that office, because of Meek's death. That would go to me. Having a legit business, Lando would be able to clean his money and we would have the best of both worlds. It was one thing left to do, and that was break Modest away from his bitch. If he had nothing left holding him here, his ass would leave.

There is no way he would question me about what happened to Meek. It was a win win situation. Smiling again, my pussy started thumping. Rubbing my pussy, I looked at Lando. He was in his feelings, but I didn't give a fuck.

"Get over here and eat this pussy. Do it right or your ass gone regret it." Knowing it was smarter to just do what I asked, he pulled my pants down and licked me good and slow.

"Don't play with me nigga. Suck my pussy like you be doing that lil ass dick. I'm ready to bust and I'm ready to do it now." Yeah I knew all about the bitch he was fucking at the club, but she was gone disappear just like his wife. I always get what the fuck I want. Starting with some fye ass head.

Damn shame it took me to mention the stripper bitch in order to get some head that I deserved. This nigga was going crazy, and I was loving it.

"Suck my ass." Without taking a second, he had his tongue going in and out of my shit and I was going crazy. Playing with my clit as he sucked my soul out, I was ready to release this shit.

"Fuck. I'm cumming baby. Lick this pussy. Mmm." My body started shaking, and I was creaming all over his face. Standing up, he started undoing his pants. "Nigga you tried it. You not hitting this pussy until I got what I want. We still have to break Modest all the way down." He was pissed, but he produced results.

"I know how to break them up." Raising my eyebrows, started to slap his ass for just now saying something, "He fuck with

June baby mama." Smiling, I knew that was a full proof plan.

There was no way they could come back from that.

"Handle it." As soon as he left out the door, my phone

rung. Not recognizing the number, I knew it was about Meek.

Getting my game face ready, I picked up.

"Hello, is this the wife of Meek Matthews?"

"Yes this is, who is this? Is something wrong?"

"His brother asked me to call you. Meek is being treated

here at the County, and he wanted you here." The fuck.

"Is he okay?"

"He is stable, but it helps when the patient has family

support." Rolling my eyes, I was pissed.

"I'm on the way." Hanging up, I had to think about that

shit. If he okay, he would tell Modest I was the one that shot him.

If he was out of it, I had a chance to finish the job. Fuck. I'll go,

but not until Lando got back. If push came to shove, he was gone

take the fall.

CHAPTER 21 MODEST

This shit was driving me crazy, and I was falling apart. Even though I didn't care for Vikki's ass, she deserved to know what was going on with her husband. For him to be at my house, I knew they had to be beefing. Right now, I was willing to put my differences to the side, maybe she could get him to respond.

Sitting here staring at him, and all these monitors had me shook. I've been sitting here since they let me back, and I was too scared to move. The doctor said talking to him could help, and I have been trying to find the right words. Resting my head against the bed, I spoke from my heart.

"When we were kids, dad talked about you all the time. I mean you could tell he was hurt, but he would always compare me to you. Boy, your brother knew better than that. Or, son that is not the way to do it. Meek ass would have never done it like that. It was hard as fuck following in your footsteps. When you stayed away, it broke him.

He would barely laugh or smile anymore, but he would always find a way to bring your name up. Even if it was in anger. When you came back, I know pops was happier than I was. He would never show it, but I know that night was the happiest he was in years. I just knew this would be the best Christmas ever.

I knew the guilt you carried from that night, but I was selfish. I was so hurt and angry, I never took your feelings into consideration. You didn't care though. No matter what I said to you, I couldn't push you away if I tried. They named you the right name. I'm sorry that I never told you thank you. I'm sorry that I never gave you the chance to help me. I acted like it didn't affect you, and I'm sorry. Even though I never said it, you helped me.

Now we are here. How the fuck could I ever get over this shit if you die on me? I need you more than you can imagine. You're my backbone, my father, my motivation. You showed me a better way, and now look at me. I'm a fucking realtor.

Meek bro I need you. Please don't leave me. You're all I have left. I know you're saying I have Malae, but I keep fucking that up. If you leave me, I won't have shit. I won't be shit. I won't make it. You're the better part of me, and I can't lose you." No

matter what I said, he didn't hear me. Wiping the tears from my

face, I leaned back and closed my eyes. I could hear Vikki before

she was in the room. Them damn heels were clacking against the

damn floor.

"How is he doing?" She looked stressed like me.

"Stable, but it's all up to him. He has to want to wake up."

She walked close to him, and grabbed his hand.

"Baby." That was all she got out before he started coding.

The doctors came running in the room, and I was losing it. For

some odd reason, Vikki didn't look sad. Out of nowhere, this girl

ran up and ran straight in the room. It was about to get bad. Before

I could stop her, because the doctors were working on him, she ran

in the room.

"Oh my God, baby I'm so sorry." They were about to ask

her to leave, but his machine started back beeping. He had come

back to us.

"She has to get the fuck out of here. This is my husband,

and I won't allow his mistress to be here with me while my

husband is fighting for her life." The girl looked pissed, but it was nothing she could do.

"Ma'am, we have to ask you to leave." The machines went crazy again, and Meek was coding. I was so nervous I was shaking. This was the scariest thing I had ever witnessed.

"Baby I'm here. Just fight for me okay. I'm here." The stranger talked again, and just like that he was stable. Now I don't believe in coincidences, and maybe I was tweaking. Whoever this chick was, is keeping Meek alive. It kind of hurt that he didn't even want to fight for me, but I was glad he was fighting. The only thing I was trying to figure out, is why he coded every time Vikki talked.

"Doc, I want to see something. Please, just stay close by in case I'm wrong. Vikki, say something to my brother." The minute she started talking, and calling him baby, he started coding. "Miss, whoever you are, can you say something please." All she said was baby, and he was stable again. "Doc, I don't know what this bitch did to my brother, but she is not allowed in here. I'm not sure what is going on, but until I figure it out, she can't come in."

"You fucking tried it, I'm his wife." The doctors asked to talk to her in the hall, and my nerves started to calm.

"Who are you?" Climbing in the bed with him, she stroked his hand as she talked to me.

"I'm Akina. Me and your brother have been seeing each other. He was leaving Vikki, but I was pissed that he went back home. He came to me that night, but I didn't let him in. Now we are here." The tears fell from her face, and I knew she was good for him. Vikki been here all this time, and not one tear fell. Seeing the love in her eyes made me think of Malae.

"Can you stay with him? If anything happens or changes, call me okay?" Giving her my number, I headed to my baby's house. She was pissed, but she always forgave a nigga. She knew I was in a bad head space and didn't mean it. I was about to knock, but I tried the door knob and it was open. She was sitting by the tree.

"Didn't I tell you to lock your doors?" When she looked up, her tears killed me. I couldn't read her, but I had a feeling it wasn't about how I talked to her. "What's wrong?" I tried to walk towards her, but she put her hand up and stopped me.

"Did you kill my baby's father?" What the fuck. I thought that nigga was already dead.

"Baby, I don't know your baby's father." Standing up, she walked over to me and stood in my face.

"DID YOU KILL MY BABY'S FATHER?" Not wanting to tell her I killed a lot of niggas in my time, I tried to figure out who the fuck was he. Drawing a blank, I had to ask her.

"Malae, who is your baby's father?" Making sure not to break eye contact with me, she stared hard.

"June." Hearing her say his name, I wanted to lie. In my heart I knew I needed to lie, but something told me she already knew. Knowing this was it for me and her, it wasn't shit I could do but tell the truth.

"Yes. He had." She cut me off.

"Five thousand dollars. You left me here struggling, crying every night over him, wiping Ty's eyes explaining to him he wasn't the reason his father left. FOR FIVE THOUSAND

DOLLARS. You're a fucking hypocrite. You out here passing out food, and giving away presents so people wouldn't make decisions out of desperation. But all of it was a lie. You did the same thing to me and Ty, that someone did to you ten years ago. YOU TOOK AWAY HIS FATHER LIKE SOMEONE TOOK AWAY YOURS. Do you know how many days we went without a meal because of his death?"

"Malae I'm sorry. Baby, please don't do this."

"Did you know?" I was confused. "Did you know I was his baby's mother?"

"Fuck no, what kind of nigga do you think I am?"

"A lying ass nigga that takes fathers away from kids, and have the nerve to sit around and cry about Christmas. Get the fuck out of my house."

"Malae, I need you. Please don't do this. Meek still haven't woke up."

"Fuck Meek, and fuck you. Let yourself out." If it had been anybody else, I would have bodied they ass. Leaving out the door, I shook my head. That was some savage ass shit to say to a nigga.

If my heart wasn't broken in a million pieces, I would have been

impressed. This had turned out to be the worse Christmas ever. Not

knowing what else to do, I drove back to the hospital. Between

Malae leaving, and my brother fighting for his life, I was on the

verge of breaking down. Something had to get better for a nigga.

CHAPTER 22 MALAE

My ass was sitting here crying my eyes out. This hurt so bad, and I didn't know how to come back from it. The worse thing that has happened in my life, was because of the nigga I was falling for. Here it was, Christmas Eve morning, and I looked a mess.

Knowing I wouldn't be able to look at Modest, there was no way I was going back to work. I'm about to be homeless, and the tree is empty as hell. My ass was so caught up in Modest and Ty bonding, I hadn't even thought about presents. If we are being honest, I assumed he would get the presents since he knew I didn't have it.

If he wasn't going through a tragedy, he would have probably still brought some stuff by. Him and Ty had gotten really close. Maybe that was me still wanting him to be some kind of good guy, but either way, that's what I told myself. We went from moving in together, to breaking up.

"Mommy, daddy Modest don't love us no more?" Hearing him call him daddy tore me apart, and now I had to help him understand it wasn't his fault.

"He does baby, but his brother was hurt bad. He has to be there for him. We may not see him for a while." Seeing him cry, made me cry with him.

"We supposed to make cookies for Santa. He promised, what did I do wrong?" Fuck, I wasn't thinking when I made this decision. It's what had to be done though. How could I stay with the nigga that killed his father? Granted he didn't know, but it didn't change the fact that he did the shit.

"I'm sorry baby, I don't know if he will be able to."

"Santa is not going to come, is he?" The parent in me wanted to lie, but I didn't want to get his hopes up. I could have easily told him we could make the cookies, but then he would be expecting gifts.

"I don't know baby." Hugging me, his tears broke my heart. This shit was hard on me, but I wanted to stand firm in my decision. Knowing Modest was at the hospital, I got Ty ready, so we could run by the office. I wanted to clean my stuff out, while he wasn't there. It would only make things worse. When we pulled up, my dumb ass forgot all that blood was out there.

"Mommy what's that?" His ass asked too many damn questions.

"It's paint." Heading inside, I made Ty sit down while I went out and cleaned it up. If Modest did come by here, it would hurt him to see this shit. Why the fuck I cared about him being hurt was beyond me. As I was scrubbing, out of nowhere it dawned on me that I never gave Lando the address. How the fuck did he know where the office was? I've been working here since they opened, and he has not come by here once.

He said he was with them when Modest killed June, if that was his best friend, why wouldn't he stop working for them. Unless, he wanted revenge. Oh my God. Running inside, I grabbed my phone. Calling Modest, his phone kept going to voicemail.

Even though we couldn't be together, I didn't want anything to happen to him. If he shot Meek, he had to be coming after Modest next. The least I could do was warn him. His voicemail picked up right away, and I left him a message. It was up to him to do what he felt best with that information. Cleaning the rest of the blood up, I went inside and got Ty. This was going to be a long sad day for him. Heading home, all I wanted to do was comfort him. Trying Modest one last time, I ended up leaving another message. If he saw it was more than one, hopefully he would check them.

"Mommy, why do all my daddies keep leaving me. Am I that bad?" Fuck. This was not a conversation I wanted to have. Hell, I didn't even know how to have it.

"Baby, Modest is not your daddy. You weren't bad Ty. Your father had to go be with the angels." Fighting back the urge to tell him, your precious Modest sent him there, I tried to explain the best way I could. "Me and Modest are friends, but sometimes friends get mad at each other. That doesn't mean he doesn't love you, it just means we aren't friends anymore."

"You made him leave and I hate you. You ruined Christmas." Jumping out of the car, he ran upstairs to the house. Not having another tear to shed, I got out and headed inside as

172

CHAPTER 23 MODEST

It was Christmas Eve, and I couldn't wait for this janky ass holiday to be over. I've been up here at the hospital every day, and there still was no change. Meek was slipping away, and it seemed only me and Akina gave a fuck. She was here the entire time, and I respected the fuck out of her. Even though they went through their differences, she put that shit aside to be here for him.

That was more than I could say for Malae's ass. She knew what this shit meant to me, and the fear I was battling with. Her ass didn't give a fuck. I could have hurt her feelings and told her the nigga June cheated on her every chance he got, but I didn't. We knew he had a girl, we just didn't know who she was. Not that it mattered, him and Lando lived in the strip club fucking the shit out of them bitches raw.

I spared her from a life of pain, but I would not use that shit as leverage. She wouldn't believe me anyway. In her head, he was on a pedestal. All she saw in me was a monster ass nigga that killed the love of her life. Even if he deserved it. Not only was he a cheating ass lying nigga, he was a fucking thief. If I had known this shit would bite me in the ass, I would have spared him. At that time, I had no idea I would be in a relationship. Everyone knew I didn't like these bitches. I used them for a nut, and that was it. My feelings were buried with my parents, until Malae.

Christmas has somehow taken away everyone I loved and cared about. Yet, everyone wanted me to like this fucked up day. This shit was for kids, and that's it. Thinking of kids, made me think of Ty. He was my lil man, and I missed his talkative ass. This shit with me and Malae was fucked up, because I made him some promises. I'm a nigga that keeps his word, and now I couldn't.

Looking over at Akina, she was just talking to Meek as if he would respond to her. The crazy part is the nigga was healing properly, he just wouldn't come back to us. The doctors said it could be the head injury that was causing this. When he fell, he hit his head, but the nigga been through worse. He was the strongest nigga I knew, and now he was here. My phone rung, and it was Vikki.

Not wanting to upset Meek, I walked out to take the call.

She had some nerve calling me. Yeah I asked her to leave, but if

that was the love of my life in there, they would have had to lock

me up every day.

"Yeah Vikki."

"How is he? Has he woken up yet?" The way that she said

it was odd to me.

"Not yet, there has been no change." She didn't cry, or

seem sad. The bitch kept talking like it was every day

conversation.

"You need to come see me. I came into some information

on who may have done this. I'm at the house, can you be here in

thirty minutes?" Looking at the phone, I decided to roll with it.

"Yeah, I'm on the way." Walking in the room, I let Akina

know I would be back. When I got in my car, my phone kept

beeping. It was voicemails from Malae. When the fuck did she

call? Pissed that I missed it, I listened as I drove. Hearing what she

told me, I knew it was something off about this shit. Laughing, I stopped by the house to get my gun. When I got back in my car, I made one more stop before I headed to go see Vikki.

****

The moment I opened the door, I knew something was off. They were used to dealing with Meek, but they underestimated me. I lived for shit like this. Meek was the thinker, the idealist. I was the enforcer, I could smell a rat a mile away. Pointing my gun behind me, I shot through the door. Making sure to aim low, I didn't want to kill them. We was about to have fun.

"Vikki, you can come out now. That shit won't work with me." Pointing my gun towards the kitchen, she came clacking out. "At least you dressed to go in the casket already. Sit the fuck down. Hey cuz, come tie this bitch up, while I get the nigga from behind the door. My cousin Blaze walked in, and you could tell he was happy as hell to be there. This nigga was retired, but I knew he wouldn't say fuck a chance at setting niggas on fire.

"Fuck you Modest."

"No bitch, fuck this stiff ass bun. Let me moisturize it for you." Blaze wasn't here two minutes, but he had already flicked

178

his Bic. That shit caught fire fast. All I could do was laugh, when he started beating her in the head trying to put it out. "Not yet lil bitch. Ain't no telling the next time I may be able to light this mother fucker." Tying Lando's bitch ass up next to Vikki, I went ahead with the questioning.

"What I want to know is what is the connection between you two." They looked at each other, but stayed silent. "Ok this is how this will work. Neither of you talk, and die in the most painful way possible. Or one of you talk, and you may save yourself." Neither said anything.

"Neither of you may know him, but I'm sure you have heard of the infamous Blaze Hoover and his Bic. You don't want to imagine the things he can do with that mother fucker. Now, if I let him go crazy, you will experience pain like never before. Is that what you want?" They looked at each other again.

"I ain't got time for this shit. Walking over to Lando, Blaze poured gas on him.

"Hold on." Lando finally spoke up. "It's all this bitch idea. She was fucking June and when he wouldn't leave his girl, she set him up. Knowing how yall treated me, she used my ass the same

way she did him. We been fucking, that's the connection." This

nigga told that shit quick.

"You're a weak ass nigga. I should have known this was

too much for your dumb ass." Vikki was three fifty hot.

"No bitch, you should have known that bun was too much.

Your neck struggling like a mother fucker to stay straight. That

mother fucker sighed when I burned half of that shit off. So, Vikki.

Let me find out that pussy woe. You around here just throwing that

thang huh Lippy?"

"Who the fuck is Lippy?" This nigga stays making up

words.

"If the hoe ain't got no walls, and all she got is lips then the

bitch is Lippy. Look, it don't matter. All that shit about to be

fucked up." This nigga was an ass.

"Who shot Meek?"

"We both did, but she did the one to his chest." Nodding

my head, I walked over to Lando like I was about to let him go. In one swift motion, I broke his neck. At least he could go quick, and

peacefully. Can't say the same for Vikki.

"Lippy, why you do it? My nigga Meek a good ass nigga.

Was it worth it?"

"He was soft, and ain't nothing worse than a weak ass man.

Talking about retiring. He ran the fucking Chi and the nigga wanna

give it up for an office." Blaze stared at her, and pulled down his

joggers. Her eyes got big, and the hoe was ready to suck his dick.

Thinking he was taking a page from Lucifer's bullshit, I stared at

this nigga in disbelief.

"Close your eyes, and open your mouth Lippy. Let's see if

your other lips any good." Smirking, she did exactly as she was

told. Leaning towards her, this nigga started pissing in her mouth.

When she realized what was going on, she started choking.

Punching her in the throat, he snatched her head back.

"Hear me good. When a nigga is smart enough to walk

away from the bullshit for his family, that doesn't make him weak.

The only thing Meek fucked up with, is marrying your sorry ass.

Finish this bitch off, she ain't even worth my fucking fluid." The fact that Blaze didn't want to set her on fire, I know he was beyond

pissed. Grabbing one of her heels, I drew my arm back and super

socked her ass. The point of it was stuck in her skin, and I wish I

could drive that bitch all the way through her head. I had never

hated someone so much in my life.

"Let's go." Blaze looked at me like I was crazy.

"You know that bitch still alive right?"

"Yeah I know. The worse thing for her would be to walk

around broke. Fuck that bitch." When we got outside, Blaze

poured the rest of his gasoline out. Before I could object, he flicked

that mother fucking Bic. The house started burning, and I just

shook my head.

"What? I know what I said, but that bitch bun bothered me.

Where the fuck he meet her ass, Sunday School? That hair and

them shoes was terrible."

"Thanks man. I'll keep you posted with Meek. He gone

fuck you up if he pulls through. All his shit in there."

"When he pulls through, and he got it. If you ain't doing shit, come swing by the house tomorrow. I know how you feel about Christmas, but you know our shit ain't normal."

"I'll let you know. Good looking."

"Hey, before you go. How did you figure it out?"

"Every time she said something, my brother coded. It was like he was trying to tell us something. Then I got a message about Lando. He wasn't smart enough to do it on his own. I put two and two together. Now get the fuck out of here before we be in jail for Christmas." We dapped up, and got the fuck out of dodge.

Heading back to the hospital, I went to check on Meek before I made my last stop.

CHAPTER 24 MALAE

Rolling over, I looked at the clock. It was Christmas Day, and all I wanted to do was go back to sleep. This was about to be hard, because Ty wasn't going to understand why he had nothing under the tree. My soul was hurting as, I pulled myself up. Going to the bathroom, I handled my hygiene. I wanted to talk to Ty before he ran out and saw it was nothing there.

Heading in his room, he was knocked out holding a Christmas book in his arms. No child should have to face the pain he was about to. He was only a kid. He didn't understand bills, and shit. Knowing I needed to get it out of the way before he woke up excited, I nudged him.

"Ty baby wake up. Come on wake up, I need to talk to you."

"Mommy is it Christmas?" Feeling my heartbreak with every second, I got ready to crush his soul.

"Yes baby, but I don't think Santa came. He told all the parents last night, that he was running behind on schedule. Some kids were going to get their presents late."

"Daddy lied to me mommy. He said Santa told him he would be here in the morning. He is going to my friend's house, why he won't come here. Mommy I promise I been good." Wiping the tears, it hurt me to know he was dreaming about June.

"Baby, it's okay. You will have all of your stuff soon. You wasn't bad, it's just coming late." Tears flooded his face.

"But daddy said if we left the cookies he would come. We made the cookies." What the hell was he talking about.

"What cookies baby? We didn't make any cookies."

"Me and daddy Modest did. He came over last night, so we could make cookies. We burned the first ones, but daddy Modest said Santa ain't want that shit. So, we made more." Laughing, I can't believe he remembered with all that he had going on.

"Watch your mouth Ty. The cookies won't make Santa come. His elves have to help him."

185

"Yes they will mommy. Watch." Knowing he was about to be heartbroken, I followed behind him. "I told you mommy. Oh my God, look at all these presents." What the fuck. Running into the front room, it was boxes everywhere. You would think a family of ten lived here. The plate that was by the tree was empty, and it was a note. Picking it up, I cried as I read it.

I meant what I said. No child should have to go through what I did. He deserves it, especially since I'm the reason he didn't have in the first place. I never break my promise, and my lil man deserves everything and more. It's a few presents for you too. Merry Christmas Malae. You have given me a new outlook, and I hope this makes up for my mistakes just a little. M

Sitting on the floor, I helped Ty open his stuff. He had game systems, a box, new tv, all kinds of toys, shoes, clothes. You name it, Ty had it. I've never seen this many gifts ever.

"Mommy Santa gave me everything on my list. This is the best Christmas ever. That one says your name mommy." Looking under the tree, I grabbed the boxes that said my name. It was a diamond necklace, bracelet, and earring set. A copy of a receipt

186

showing my rent was paid up, and the last box was some keys. Not

knowing what they were too, I didn't think anything of it.

"Mommy can we go tell daddy Modest?" Knowing the

right thing to do was say thank you, we got dressed and headed out

the door. My car was gone, and it was another one in its spot. What

the fuck. Running downstairs, it was a 2018 White BMW truck. It

was an envelope on the dash. Me and Ty, got in and my ass was

crying hard now.

"Mommy did you ask Santa for a new car?" Laughing, I

didn't know what to say.

"I guess so baby." Opening the envelope, it was a check for

ten thousand dollars, and a note.

I'm the reason you had to struggle, so it's only right I make

sure you never struggle again. No rent, and no car note. That

check is what I got from the old car. Since you refuse to lock your

doors, I'll drop by every month to leave something and make sure

you're straight. M

How the fuck do you stay mad at someone who not only

thought of you, but your son as well why he was in his darkest times? This man touched my heart, and just had to see him. Flying to the hospital, I damn near drug Ty upstairs. The girl Akina was lying in the bed with Meek, and Modest was sitting there staring into space.

"Daddy Modest." The way Ty snatched away from me and ran to him, made me feel like shit. Modest was just as happy to see him as well.

"Daddy Modest, I'm glad we threw those other cookies away. Santa came and ate all the ones we made. He brought me everything I wanted, and more. He must have really liked those cookies."

"I told you my cookies was special." All I could do was smile at them.

"Can you make the cookies every year? I don't think he likes mommy's cookies. He has never brought this much stuff."

"You got it lil man." He finally looked at me, and I could tell he was nervous. "Merry Christmas Malae." Walking over to him, I stared in his eyes. The hurt, the remorse, his love for me, all showed in his eyes. Leaning forward, I kissed him softly on the lips.

"Merry Christmas Modest." Finally turning towards the bed, I hugged Akina. "Merry Christmas boo." Finally, I bent down and hugged Meek. "Merry Christmas Mr. Matthews." Me and Modest laughed.

"Merry Christmas." Everybody head snapped around and looked at Meek. The fuck. "I better have some gifts and shit, and not that cheap shit either." We all forgot he was shot, and piled on top of him. "Yeah, yeah I love yall too. Can yall give me five minutes to talk to my brother?"

"No need. It was already handled. Merry Christmas nigga. Now if you don't mind, I need to go ummm tip and dip my girl real quick." My pussy jumped, and he didn't have to tell me twice.

"Nasty bitch." Laughing at Meek, me and Modest was on the way to my house since it was closer.

"Ty, daddy need you to do me a favor when we get home. Play in your room, and don't come out until daddy comes and get you okay?" Trying not to laugh, I know Ty wanted him all to his self.

"Okay, I'll play my game." This nigga damn near ran into the gate when we turned into the lot. As soon as we got inside, he made sure Ty was straight and then it was grown up time. Locking the door, he slammed me against it. Rubbing his fingers against my clit through my leggings, it was hard to talk.

"I'm sorry I wasn't able to get you anything for Christmas."

"You gave me more than I could ever imagine. Now shut the fuck up and let me in." Kicking my legs apart, he leaned down and pulled my pants down. "You been in the shower right?"

"Nigga stop playing."

"You know I'm new to this shit. Don't want to fuck it up by eating some day old pussy." Before I could respond, his mouth covered my clit.

"Damn I missed you." Sliding his fingers in my ass while he ate my pussy, I creamed in twenty seconds flat. My body was shaking, and I couldn't wait for him to get inside of me. Snatching me to the bed, he took his clothes off.

"Come ride this dick." The look on my face showed him I wanted him to beat my back in. "You thought I was playing. Your ass about to get this tip and dip. A nigga tired, and you about to do all the work. You ain't never heard about that lazy fuck Modest?" Laughing, I slid on top of him.

"Shut up." Pushing me down on him hard, he groaned and shook a little.

"Ride this dick baby." And my horny ass did just that.

EPILOGUE

AKINA...

Never would I have ever thought that I would find love again. Not searching and not looking, all I wanted was to stay connected to my daughter. Meek came in like a thief in the night, and stole my heart, body, and soul.

I've never considered myself to be a homewrecker, but I believe that me and Meek crossed paths for a reason. I needed him, and without being asked, he gave me that and then some. It's rare finding a man with the morals and values that he has, but I did and I'm never letting his ass go.

When I thought I lost him, it felt like Gabbie all over again. I would never make that mistake again. On the 12th day of Christmas my savage gave to me, healing, and love. That was all that a girl like me needed.

MEEK...

Ain't nothing worse than thinking you was dying, and on the way to that upper room When Jesussss. A nigga really thought it was over, but to see the woman that was supposed to love you pull the trigger, that shit does something to your mental.

When I opened my eyes, doubt crossed my mind for a brief moment. What if she was like Vikki? How do I know she is not a fraud? Then I remembered how I felt when she walked away from me. Even if this was not where I was supposed to be, I knew that it was where I wanted to be.

She made me feel like no woman has ever done. She was there the entire time my brother was, and a nigga knew deep down she was the one. Glad to know my brother handled them bitch ass mother fuckers, I could move on. I wouldn't marry right away, but I knew she was my forever. On the 12th day of Christmas my baby gave to me, true love.

MELAE...

Had anyone told me I could be with the nigga that killed who I thought was my true love, I would have slapped they ass to sleep. Not only was I with him, but I was gone off that nigga. Ty no longer calls him daddy Modest, it's just daddy now. Not once has he ever corrected him. I asked Modest why did he kill June, and all he said was "It was all on me. No excuses." I know that's not true, but the fact that he loved me enough to spare my feelings, meant a lot to me.

Even though he had paid the rent up on my place, me and Ty moved in with Modest. Even when my ass wanted a break, Ty wouldn't allow me too. Money wise, I wasn't able to buy him anything for Christmas, but I gave him much more. This nigga was everything and he was mine. On the 12th day of Christmas my savage gave to me, a father to my child. He saved me when I was at my lowest. He saw me when I felt invisible. He loved me.

194

MODEST...

A nigga never thought the day, he could look at Christmas and say it was the best day of my life. Malae forgave a nigga, and I have never been happier. My brother woke up, and he also has true love. There was no way I thought I would be here after barging in her house to curse her trifling ass out.

My lil man gave me so much life, and it wasn't until him that I ever thought about having a kid. That lil nigga loved me like he came from my nut sack, and I will never treat him like he didn't. After everything I had lost on that day, I ended up gaining so much more. Malae was what a nigga needed, and my girl was what I wanted. She changed me, and I'm man enough to know it. On the 12th day of Christmas my girl gave to me, a healed heart, a son, and in eight months, a baby of our own. A nigga around here feeling real good. Merry Christmas from my family to yours. Turn the page to read about the Hoover Gang Christmas. The End.

A HOOVER GANG CHRISTMAS

Blaze

"Loosey, are you done with the food? Everybody about to show up in minute. Your ass always late." She grabbed Spark and rolled her eyes.

"If you got your bad ass daughter, I could finish. Her ass into every fucking thing."

"If your ass was done, she could open her damn presents. Just hurry up, I'm ready to see what you got me. I'm about to let her open one. Come here daddy's baby, Let's open one."

"Yay. Presents." Laughing, I grabbed her and took her to the tree.

"You can open one of the ones daddy got you." Handing her a small box. She started tearing off the paper. Drea crazy ass was standing there with her camera, ready to take pics when her ass supposed to be cooking. When the paper came all the way off,

Spark ass went crazy. She was happy as hell, and I knew that would be her favorite gift.

"Blaze. Why the fuck did you get our daughter a pack of lighters for Christmas?" My wife was mad as hell, but I knew what my baby girl wanted.

"So she can stop stealing my shit. I bet she don't like no other gift better than mine? You wanna bet." Smacking her teeth, she headed towards the kitchen. "Mommy knows what's up." The doorbell rung, and the guests were starting to arrive. Nobody had opened any presents. All of it was at my house, and we agreed to do Christmas here. I'm sure the kids were mad and ready to open their shit.

"Hey uncle Blaze." Zavi ass was getting big, and I don't see how he could get anything. That lil nigga was so spoiled, he had everything. Hugging Quick and Ash, I let them in. Not getting a chance to close the door, Babyface, Juicy, and Zaria was walking in.

We all stood around talking shit, until the doorbell rang again. My mama and Devon walked in, and Kimmie stormed past us like this was her shit.

"Hold the fuck on, you too damn big to be pushing past people and shit. Where the fuck my chest hair go? You ate my shit? Gotta watch her ass, she eats quick." Her ass stayed mad all the time. Shadow must not be feeding her ass.

"Nigga if you don't watch your nasty ass mouth. You the only trifling mother fucker I know that talks like a pastor ain't in the room." Me and Devon looked at my mama like she lost her damn mind. Walking in the house, I was not for her shit.

"Ma, your wig looking kind of woe, you need me to buy you some for Christmas?"

"Fuck you, I got a quickie in the car. That ain't shit but a lil sweat."

"So, sweat make your shit look like a sheep dog?"

"Blaze, not today. Go sit your slow ass down. Spark, come give granny a hug." Heading back over to Quick and Face, I needed to know what the fuck was going on.

"Where the fuck is Shadow?"

"That nigga stay disappearing. I think he got another plus one or some shit. Anytime we doing something, he ain't never around. Kimmie be hot as hell." Quick was on point, but it still didn't tell us where he was.

"Apparently not hot enough. Sweat supposed to make you lose weight. She barged her ass in here and damn near took my nipple off."

"Blaze, it's Christmas and her husband is not here. Can you give her a break?" Ignoring his question, we needed to figure out what was going on with our baby brother.

"We need to call a meeting. Whatever is going on with this nigga, we have to figure it out. Not today though. It's Christmas, and I'm not trying to ruin my shit.

"Aww hell naw. If yall don't get this seed of chucky, I'm gone fuck her up. This mother fucker done burnt up my good wig." Turning around, my mama was screaming because Spark used her new Christmas gift, and set my mama wig on fire. She was beating the hell out of that thang.

199

"You just like your damn daddy. Get your ass away from me. Who the fuck gave this baby a lighter?" Knowing my mama was gone be pissed, I ignored her.

"Loosey can you get Spark?"

"Why the fuck you are calling her Loosey?" As mama say, for his name to be Quick, sometimes his ass was slow.

"Got tired of calling her Loose pussy. Shortened that shit."

"How the fuck I'm supposed to cook, and get Spark?" Drea was snapping off.

"Loosey mad." Spark didn't know when to leave shit alone. Laughing, I grabbed her.

"Hush girl before your mama put me on punishment." My brothers laughed, and I prayed Drea didn't hold off tonight. It was Christmas, and I was looking forward to that shit.

"Your mama over there mad as hell, keep Spark away from her." When Face said that, we looked over and mama had the wig back on her head, and smoke was coming off that bitch. Not wanting to get cursed out, we laughed to ourselves and tried to change the subject.

"Babyface, you can gone and sing your song while we waiting on the food." I was trying my best to keep Spark from getting a whooping. When I did that shit years ago, mama whooped me for days.

"Awww shit. I'm ready for this." Quick snatches Ash up fast as hell.

"Let me find out you trying to slip on that nigga dick too. You can't hang with Drea no more unless I'm there. I'll shoot that nigga in his shin." Face looked at me praying I wasn't on no bullshit. Every time they bring it up, I do something to his ass. Standing in front of everybody, he started singing.

"Oh holy night, the stars are brightly shining. It is the night of our dear Savior's birth. Long lay the world in sin and error pining."

"Hold the on. What the fuck is you singing. If your simple ass don't sing some black shit or a song everybody knows. Dumb ass singing about a hoe in the night." We laughed at mama, but I agreed. I had no idea what this nigga was singing about. Shaking his head, he changed the song.

"Hang all the mistletoes, I'm going to get to know you

better. This Christmas, and as we trim the tree, how much fun it's

gonna be together. This Christmas. The fireside is blazing bright,

we're caroling through the night. And this Christmas, will be a

very special Christmas for me." We all stood around while this

skinny ass nigga sung like a mother fucker. That nigga could sing

his ass off though.

I was sitting there smiling like a fool, when I felt the heat

on my face. What the fuck. No this lil girl didn't. Dropping her to

the floor, I ran to the mirror.

"Blaze why you drop that girl like that?" Not wanting to

answer Babyface, I knew they ass was gone laugh all night.

"This mother fucker burned my damn mustache. I'm

fucking you up Spark." She took off running, and my brothers

shielded her.

"Nigga you look like a pedophile uncle." This nigga Face

had jokes already.

"And your mama looks like burnt gyro meat. What you saying? I almost told you to sing Mary had a little lamb. Rough ass wig."

"Fuck you bitch, at least I can still wear my shit. Where your mustache at empty lip?" Looking at Spark I wanted to football kick her ass. Everybody was in tears, but I had a trick for they ass. They thought the shit was all ha ha and hee hees. Ain't no fuck when Blaze got the gun. Heading in the kitchen, we sat down and ate. Keeping quiet, I waited for my turn to get all they ass back.

"Okay kids, yall ready to open your presents?"

"Yeeesssss." That shit was music to my ears. Glad Drea asked that, I knew me, and my baby was on the same page.

"Blaze go light the tree up." Smiling I went to the front room with them on my ass. The kids were jumping up and down, the grown ups were excited, and I was over the fucking moon. Walking up to the tree, I flicked my mother fucking Bic. The tree and presents caught fire quick as hell.

"Nigga are you crazy. Why the fuck would you do that dumb ass shit?" Quick was mad, and everybody stared on in disbelief. My ass played dumb.

"What? How yall gone ask a nigga with a fire problem to light the tree. What the fuck yall thought I was gone do? Who the fuck plugs a tree up in the daylight?"

"Naw nigga, who the fuck sets the damn tree on fire. I swear your ass do the most." Face was getting mouthy like he forgot.

"Excuse me come again say what?"

"Get the damn fire extinguisher."

"I thought that's what you said. Merry Christmas mother fuckers."

KEEP UP WITH LATOYA NICOLE

Like my author page on fb @misslatoyanicole

My fb page Latoya Nicole Williams

IG Latoyanicole35

Twitter Latoyanicole35

Snap Chat iamTOYS

Reading group: Toy's House of Books

OTHER BOOKS BY LATOYA NICOLE

NO WAY OUT: MEMOIRS OF A HUSTLA'S GIRL

NO WAY OUT 2: RETURN OF A SAVAGE

GANGSTA'S PARADISE

GANGSTA'S PARADISE 2: HOW DEEP IS YOUR LOVE

ADDICTED TO HIS PAIN (STANDALONE)

LOVE AND WAR: A HOOVER GANG AFFAIR

LOVE AND WAR 2: A HOOVER GANG AFFAIR

LOVE AND WAR 3: A HOOVER GANG AFFAIR

LOVE AND WAR 4: A GANGSTA'S LAST RIDE

CREEPING WITH THE ENEMY: A SAVAGE STOLE MY HEART

I GOTTA BE THE ONE YOU LOVE (STANDALONE)

THE RISE AND FALL OF A CRIME GOD: PHANTOM AND ZARIA'S STORY

THE RISE AND FALL OF A CRIME GOD 2: PHANTOM AND ZARIA'S STORY

TO MY READERS

BOOK 15, AND I CAN'T BELIEVE IT. TWO NUMBER ONES,

I'M STILL IN DISBELIEF. YOU GUYS ARE AWESOME, AND

I LOVE YOU. THANK YOU FOR CONTINOUSLY MAKING

MY BOOKS A SUCCESS. WITHOUT YOU THERE IS NO ME.

MAKE SURE YOU DOWNLOAD, SHARE, READ AND

REVIEW. MORE BOOKS WILL BE COMING FROM ME. BE

ON THE LOOK OUT. MLPP WE BRINGING THE HEAT.

CPSIA information can be obtained
at www.ICGtesting.com
Printed in the USA
LVOW13s1935140218
566611LV00018B/445/P